The silence thickened. She waited for him to say something, he supposed. But his mind wasn't on talking at the moment. The electricity zinging between them was burning him up.

Finally she looked up at him. "I never get involved with employees." The need blazing in her eyes protested the statement.

"Technically, I'm not an employee." His voice was husky. He wanted to touch her but didn't dare. He, too, had a rule against getting involved with a client...but technically she wasn't his client.

"Guess not," she agreed. She licked those lush lips again. "Truth is, I haven't been kissed in more than three years. I may have forgotten how it's done."

He reached out and removed the clip that held her hair. He wanted her to feel what a kiss from the right man felt like.

DEBRA WEBB

HIGH NOON

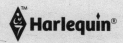
TORONTO NEW YORK LONDON
AMSTERDAM PARIS SYDNEY HAMBURG
STOCKHOLM ATHENS TOKYO MILAN MADRID
PRAGUE WARSAW BUDAPEST AUCKLAND

To my family, for always being there for me.

Recycling programs
for this product may
not exist in your area.

ISBN-13: 978-0-373-74675-0

HIGH NOON

Copyright © 2012 by Debra Webb

ABOUT THE AUTHOR

Debra Webb wrote her first story at age nine and her first romance at thirteen. It wasn't until she spent three years working for the military behind the Iron Curtain and within the confining political walls of Berlin, Germany, that she realized her true calling. A five-year stint with NASA on the space shuttle program reinforced her love of the endless possibilities within her grasp as a storyteller. A collision course between suspense and romance was set. Debra has been writing romance, suspense and action-packed romance thrillers since. Visit her at www.debrawebb.com or write to her at P.O. Box 4889, Huntsville, AL 35815.

Books by Debra Webb

CAST OF CHARACTERS

Joel Hayden—He has plenty of experience providing protection, but everything about this case is different. How do you protect a woman who doesn't realize she's in danger?

Laney Seagers—She's used to taking care of herself and her son. With her son's father giving her trouble—not to mention the bank calling in her loan—the last thing she needs is a new kind of trouble in her life.

Buddy Seagers—He's five years old and the light of Laney's life.

Terry Kingston—The only person he really cares about is him. But he needs his son to stay in his wealthy father's good graces. How far is he willing to go to make that happen?

Janet Tolliver—She holds the key to many dark, dangerous secrets.

Rafe and Clare Barker—The Princess Killers. Which of them is really the cold-blooded murderer? The one on death row or the one recently released?

Tony Weeden—Who is he loyal to? Rafe? Clare? Or himself?

Victoria Colby-Camp—She and Lucas are supposed to be retired, but there is something about this case that just won't let them go.

Lucas Camp—He fears Victoria is being drawn into an emotional war that no one can win.

Simon Ruhl—The head of the new Colby, Texas, agency.

Chapter One

Beaumont, Texas,
Sunday, May 26th, 9:50 p.m.

Joel Hayden had lingered in a dark corner of the High Noon Saloon for the past two hours. Finally a patron vacated a stool at the bar and Joel settled there before anyone else in the happy crowd could commandeer the prized position.

Whatever Laney Seagers was doing, she was doing it right. The century-old tavern she'd resurrected with her own two hands was hopping even on a Sunday night. The music flowing from the jukebox was country all the way and the atmosphere pure Texas from the murals on the walls depicting one-horse towns from the West's heyday when duels were carried out in the street at high noon to the restored original wood floor that had seen its share of two-stepping boots and bloody brawls. The patrons carried the mood with their cowboy boots and Stetsons.

He'd watched Laney Seagers for the past three days. Wasn't a hardship. The lady made his job easy, a vacation almost. Each time she laughed, the sound, sultry and sexy, left every single male customer within hearing range slack-jawed. Her honey-blond hair swung around her shoulders, making his fingers itch to see if it felt as silky as it looked.

Joel had handled a generous list of personal protection gigs for businessmen, celebrities and politicians alike, but he had to admit, this one was different. His new employer, the Colby Agency, wanted those with the most experience in the field on this case. This was Joel's first assignment for the Colby Agency and not one to be taken lightly, despite the spirited setting and the sexy blonde in the tight jeans and formfitting T-shirt sporting the saloon's logo.

Laney Seagers was in danger. And that was the easy part. That she didn't realize the threat nipping at her heels was the element that made the situation less than optimal. Though Joel would rather watch the lady scurry around behind the bar than eat at chow time, there was only so much even the most highly trained bodyguard could do under the circumstances.

Throw in the mix a five-year-old kid who

was scared to death of his own shadow and things were a little complicated. Since the boy wouldn't start kindergarten until the fall, he spent most of his time attached to his pretty mother's hip. Even now, as she worked the Sunday-night crowd, Buddy slept on a cot in the office. Whenever he was awake, he played video games in the kitchen where the cook, Tatum, a landlocked former sailor he called Uncle Tater, kept him company. Every other moment he clung to his mom. Thing was, the kid didn't play just any old kind of games; they were the learning kind, reading, math and the like. As seemingly introverted as he was, little Buddy Seagers was as smart as a whip.

Joel had three brothers and they had all grown up hard. Their mother had developed multiple sclerosis when Joel was about Buddy's age. By the time he was ten, she was helpless. Their father had been busy trying to keep a roof over their heads and food on the table. Later, when Joel was older, he also understood that it was easier for his dad to work all the time than to come home to an ever-unfolding tragedy.

Basically, the Hayden boys pretty much learned to take care of themselves out of necessity. Made Joel wonder if shy little Buddy had a chance against the bullies he would face in school. Without a proper father figure or even an older brother, preparing him to take care of himself fell on the mother's shoulders. He didn't know many mothers who taught their boys how to land a nice uppercut.

It wasn't really his business whether or not Laney Seagers was up to that particular challenge, but being a kid from a primarily one-parent household, he wondered. She sure seemed to take by the horns the other challenges life tossed her way. Her background reflected a tough lady who preferred being a survivor to being a victim. A guy had to respect that. Rather than rely on entitlements, she got out and made things happen.

Laney sashayed over to where he sat at the center of the long counter. She smiled that big, bright smile that made her brown eyes twinkle and left a man a little dazed, and then she glanced at his half-empty glass.

"Somehow you just don't look like a soda pop kinda guy to me, handsome. Can I get you something else?"

"I have a one-drink limit when I'm doing the driving home." He gifted her with a wink and a smile of his own. "Unless you're planning on taking me home, I guess it'll be soda for me the rest of the night."

She belted out another of those sultry laughs.

"I have to give you credit, that's the first time I've heard that one." She picked up his glass. "You having regular or diet?"

There went that dazzling twinkle in her eyes again.

Beyond the fact that she was a knockout with a killer smile and inspiring eyes, he genuinely liked the lack of pretention in her manner and her looks. No fussy makeup or hairdos. She seemed completely comfortable in her own skin. He liked that a lot. She had spirit in spite of the hard luck she'd survived.

"Regular."

She filled his glass and placed it on a fresh napkin in front of him. "We've still got wings and ribs in the kitchen," she suggested.

He held up a hand. "I'm good."

"You don't know what you're missing."

Watching her walk away wasn't in his job description, at least not the part where he zeroed in on those tight-fitting jeans. But then he was only human. Any woman who looked that good in plain old denim deserved a long, lustful stare from any man breathing.

Since this was work, there was very little chance he would have the opportunity to see what he was missing beyond watching her swing those hips. That alone was worth hanging around twenty-four/seven for however long it took.

Tonight, if all went as planned, he'd get his opportunity to get a little closer. He'd overheard the one remaining member of her security make the statement that he wasn't getting paid enough to deal with the boss's ex. The frustrated guy intended to give Laney the bad news tonight. He'd already accepted another position with the competition downtown and he wasn't feeling inclined to give even a one-week notice.

A lot of that had been happening this week.

A raw deal for Laney but a much-needed opportunity for Joel to gain a better surveillance position. He'd laid the necessary groundwork with subtle comments to some of Laney's employees.

He swiveled on the stool, his back against the counter, and surveyed the crowd. At a table near the jukebox, a belligerent and clearly inebriated jerk annoyed the waitress attempting to take his order. From a distance he appeared your average had-a-little-too-much reveler. But that was far from the case.

He was the rub. The no-good baby daddy himself. Terrence "Terry" Kingston. Poster boy for thirty-something men with failure-to-launch syndrome. And missing in action ninety percent of the time for the past five years under the guise of finishing his law degree so he could follow in his rich daddy's footsteps. Though he and Laney had never married, he was the father of her son.

A self-absorbed, egotistical leech who just wanted to play from time to time with the one girl smart enough to walk away. His serial stints in rehab had prevented him from taking legal action to obtain partial custody of his son. Not that he'd actually wanted the responsibility but the threat worked well when he wanted something else from Laney. Knowing the kind of money his father had put Laney at a serious disadvantage. Fear had likely prevented her from taking legal steps to get the guy out of her life once and for all.

But now Kingston had a new motive. Rich daddy had cut off his trust fund after the last round of detox following his son's surrender to his never-quite-relinquished relationship with cocaine. So slacker Kingston junior needed a way back into rich daddy's good graces. A brief background check and a few questions asked of the right folks and Joel had the whole sordid story.

There was nothing like a grandson, an heir, from an only son—an opportunity for a do-over—to get rich daddy's attention. The desire to do it right this time, with a grandson when he obviously failed with his only son, was a powerful persuader for a man marching toward sixty. The senior Kingston had built his empire with no time for anything else and the guilt had caught up with him.

Kingston junior, on the other hand, was banking on his five-year-old investment to get his fingers back in the money jar.

And Joel was counting on human nature.

The cocky man swaggered up to the bar, his right tilt giving away his increasing level of intoxication. He elbowed aside a couple of patrons and bellied up to the counter. The unhappy folks grumbled but walked away rather than risk trouble.

The exchange between the ex and the saloon owner was muted by the lively music roaring from the jukebox, but Joel didn't need to hear the words to get the gist of the conversation. The body language of both participants telegraphed the story loud and clear to anyone who bothered to look.

He wanted something and she wasn't having any part of it.

Dekker, the security detail for the night—and every night since Joel's arrival—cut through the crowd and stationed himself next to the troublemaker. Dekker was a big guy. Six-three or four. Two-forty or two-fifty. Looked like a linebacker for a pro football team.

Joel finished off his soda and stood. Things were about to get interesting and he didn't want to miss the show.

Kingston turned on the big guy wearing the High Noon Saloon T-shirt and whatever he said didn't sit well. Dekker turned to Laney, shook his head and walked out.

Based on the gossip Joel had heard from the waitresses, Dekker was sick of throwing Kingston out night after night and getting nowhere. The local cops wouldn't give the guy what he deserved for fear of reprisals from his rich daddy. Adding to the pressure, Kingston had started threatening Dekker's wife's position at one of the elementary schools. Old man Kingston had friends in high places, the smart-mouthed jerk liked to brag.

Well, Joel didn't care who his daddy was or where his friends fell on the food chain. He just wanted to kick the crap out of him on principle.

By the time Joel made his way down to that end of the bar, the patrons had scattered and Laney and Kingston were going at it loud enough to drown out the music.

A few more minutes and they would successfully clear the house. Bad for business.

And Joel happened to know Laney couldn't afford any dips in revenue.

"You can't keep me from seeing my son," Kingston slurred. "I'm petitioning the court for full custody. My daddy says this time I'll win. And you can't do a damned thing but co-operate or forfeit."

"Do what you think you're big enough to do," she dared. "Until then, you can see Buddy when you're sober and only when you're sober. Right now, I want you out of here. This is my property and I have the right to kick your drunken butt out if you can't behave."

The arrogant fool laughed. "The way I hear it, that may be changing very soon. Money makes the world go round, in case you haven't learned that yet."

Laney was fighting mad. But beneath all that bravado she was terrified. Didn't take a degree in psychology to see that. She wore her emotions on her sleeve. It worked for her because they were honest, no-drama emotions. Something else Joel liked about her.

"I thought I might go for bourbon after all. Straight up," Joel said as he cozied up to the bar next to the sleazebag harassing the lady.

Laney took a breath, shifted her attention to him. "Sure." She pivoted and stalked over to the rows of liquor bottles lining the mirrored shelves behind the bar.

"Who the hell are you?" Kingston glared at Joel, his bleary eyes reporting his alcohol-consumption level better than any breathalyzer could.

Joel leaned closer to the man and said for his ears only, "I'm the guy who's going to ruin those new veneers your daddy's money bought if you don't leave the lady alone and get the hell out of here."

Kingston reared back, swayed. He patted his pocket. "Old switch might have something to say about that."

Joel grabbed him by the collar, lifted him just high enough to prevent his boots from settling square on the floor, and hauled him across the room and out the swinging doors.

The drunken SOB cursed and swung repeatedly at Joel, missing every time. Joel snagged the key ring from the weasel's belt and shoved him away. "If you have any friends, call someone to pick you up. Otherwise, call a cab."

The guy charged at him. Joel stepped aside. Kingston went down face-first on the wooden walkway created as authentically as the ones straight out of an old Western movie. In fact, the whole scene could have been out of a classic John Wayne movie. Except Laney wore those body-hugging jeans instead of an ankle-length dress and petticoats.

"Show your face in here again," Joel warned, "and I won't be so nice next time."

Joel waited at the door until Kingston staggered away, cell at his ear, hopefully calling for a ride.

Joel turned around and came face-to-face with the boss.

"Is he gone?"

"For now." Joel glanced over his shoulder. "He'll be back eventually for his ride." He passed the keys to her.

"I wish that was the only reason for him to come back." She stared across the parking lot, probably hoping the bastard would fade into the darkness never to be seen again.

"You okay?" The question wasn't necessary. He could see that she was far from okay, but she had no way of knowing he understood far too keenly the unappealing facts of her financial and personal situations.

She shrugged, threw the bar towel over her shoulder. "I'd be a lot better if my security hadn't bailed on me. That really blows."

Joel made a show of considering the idea for a moment. "Maybe it is my lucky night."

Her eyebrows shot up in skepticism. "Look, mister, your pickup lines will have to get a lot better than what I've heard so far for you to get lucky." She looked him up and down. "Packaging isn't everything."

Joel laughed. "I wasn't referring to that kind of luck, ma'am."

Her cheeks flushed. She hitched a thumb toward the swinging doors. "I have to get back in there. Without someone keeping an eye on the crowd, anything could happen."

She had no idea. The Kingston men were just the beginning of her troubles. As frustrating as things were for her at the moment, he hated to eventually be the one to let her know that it was going to get a lot worse before it got better.

He gave her a nod. "If you decide to hire a new bouncer, let me know. I'm in the market for a new job."

Joel tipped his hat to her and stepped down from the walkway. He'd taken another two strides when she called out to him.

"How can I get in touch with you?"

He turned to face her, backed up another step. "I'm right here." He shrugged. "I'll probably be back tomorrow night."

"You'd have to fill out an application."

He paused.

For a lady who wanted to play it tough, she looked damned vulnerable at the moment. But then he knew why. Couldn't blame her for feeling that and more.

"I'd need references," she tacked on.

"I can handle that."

She hitched her head toward the door then disappeared inside. Joel followed, enjoying the view. Wasn't often that the backside was every bit as gorgeous as the front, but this lady was definitely all-around gorgeous.

His job was to protect all of her and he finally had his in. Being employed at the High Noon would make his work a whole lot easier.

She skirted the end of the bar and poured that bourbon he'd had to walk away from. When she set the drink on the counter, she grabbed a pen and a napkin and placed them in front of him.

He glanced from the napkin and pen to her.

"The application. Just jot down the usual stuff. Name, address, phone number and references. I need their numbers, too. Use both sides if necessary."

"Yes, ma'am." Joel scrawled the requested info on the napkin. He flipped it over and provided a couple of names with numbers he retrieved from his cell. When he'd added the final digit, he passed it to her.

"Anything else?"

She studied the information. "When can you start?"

He grinned. "I thought I already had."

She tried to look serious but one of those breath-stealing smiles peeked past her cautionary business persona. "All right. The pay is a percentage of the night's take. It's nothing to brag about some nights, but others make up for it."

"Works for me."

"I will call your references," she reminded him.

"Then you'll really be impressed."

She held his gaze a moment. "We'll see."

Chapter Two

Laney perched on the edge of her son's bed and watched him sleep all snuggled up with his bear. He'd had that ragged old thing since he was born. It was the first toy she'd bought her child. She'd walked into the gift shop and immediately been drawn to the cute brown bear with its red bow tie. Made her feel safe and it seemed to do the same thing for Buddy. As silly as that sounded.

Regret settled heavily onto her shoulders. These late nights were hard on him. She had hoped to have a good solid staff on board before school started in late August so she could get her boy home at a decent hour, but with Dekker's abrupt departure that was looking less and less likely.

Last week it had been two waitresses.

What was she going to do?

Getting home after midnight on Sunday night—a school night come this fall—was not going to work. She had to get a good team in place soon.

Terry was running off all her best help. The police would do nothing for fear of a backlash from his father. How did you fight that kind of trouble?

After all these years, why in hell did he have to hunt her down now? She hadn't seen the bastard but twice in five years. Both times he'd been looking for a place to crash when things got too hot for him in Houston. Which generally meant his father had gotten fed up and decided to actually act like a father. Too little too late, unfortunately for both Terry and her.

She'd let him fool her the first time, but not the second. He'd been furious when she wouldn't let him into the little apartment she'd had at the time or into her bed. The Kingston men weren't used to hearing no for an answer.

They weren't kids anymore. The time for playing games was over. She had a home and a business, as well as a son about to start school. She had responsibilities that needed her full attention and her best efforts. Terry needed to grow up.

Laney might have gotten a rough start with her life, but she was a quick learner. She was a bit of a sap but she was no dummy. The idea of allowing her mistakes to damage her son's future hurt too much to even think about.

She tucked the covers around her baby, gave him a kiss and checked the window by his bed. Locked, shade drawn. Relieved the day was mostly done, she made her way to the kitchen. There hadn't been time for even a five-minute break tonight, which was a good thing for her bank account. Now, however, her stomach was demanding attention.

As she took sandwich fixings from the fridge and deposited them on the worn wooden counter of her makeshift island, she considered that tomorrow she had to hire at least one of the new waitresses she needed. And she'd have to check the references on her new security guy.

Her fingers slowed in their work. Joel Hayden had been hanging around most of the week. One of the waitresses had told her he'd recently gotten laid off from his work as a bodyguard at some swanky security company that had closed its doors. Jobs were tough to come by these days and he'd opted to take a break from Houston's big-city noise and mayhem. Beaumont, he insisted to the waitress who was clearly enamored with him, fit the bill.

Part of her couldn't help thinking that it was

not a coincidence that he hailed from Houston.
Terry and his family were Houstonians. But,
after the way Hayden had rousted her ex out of
the saloon, she figured that wasn't very likely.
Unless the whole scene had been staged.

Damn. She hadn't thought of that until now.
Great. Something else to worry about. Maybe
she'd do some checking beyond his references.
Google him or something.

After stuffing two slices of bread with ham,
cheese, mayo and tomato, she grabbed a beer
and found her favorite spot in the living room.
Her little corner on the sofa. Most of the living room served as a play area for Buddy. He
had his Legos in one corner. His game station
in another. And miscellaneous toys in yet another. At five, the kid was already more organized than most adults. He kept Laney on the
straight and narrow when it came to clutter.

He was so smart that he scared her sometimes. Not in a bad way, though. Her biggest
fear was that she would never be able to provide him with the opportunities he deserved.
College tuition was outrageous. She had already started saving for that but it wasn't much
to speak of. She had thirteen years and so far
her math was way off reaching the necessary
sum.

"That plan's really holding together," she

muttered. Between the walk-in cooler in the High Noon's kitchen going out and that fancy automatic toaster oven Tatum had insisted he needed to make sandwiches folks would love, the almighty dollar was tough to hang on to.

Laney sighed as she settled into her corner. She clicked the remote and set the station to a movie channel that featured classic love stories. What could she say? She had to get her happily-ever-afters from somewhere. And there was nothing like getting lost in a sappy movie after a long, hard night at the High Noon.

Truthfully, she couldn't complain. Her life had sucked for a while after her parents died. The accident had devastated her entire life. Just a ten-year-old kid with no relatives to take her in. Foster care hadn't been so bad, but Laney had. She'd been a pain in the butt until she was eighteen and then she'd been an idiot.

As stupid as she was and as many mistakes as she had made, she had a beautiful son because of at least one of those errors in judgment. She couldn't regret Buddy.

Man, she hadn't realized how starved she was. Something as simple as a ham and cheese sandwich shouldn't have a girl moaning but Laney had learned enjoying the simple things in life came with the single-mom territory.

As a single mom and a business owner,

there was rarely any time left for a social life. Hayden's image tried to nudge its way into her thoughts.

Hayden was business. She had to keep that fact firmly in front of her. He had trouble written all over that sexy frame.

She gave herself another fifteen minutes of me time before reluctantly moving on to the other chores that would not be put off. Laundry, dishes. Forget about picking up around the house. She was way too exhausted.

Her hodgepodge kitchen wasn't exactly state-of-the-art. Far from it actually. She'd spent the past two years scrounging for cast-offs from folks remodeling their kitchens. Few of the cabinets matched; none of the appliances were the same color or from the same decade, but they all had one thing in common—they worked! Even Tatum saw the beauty in her vision when it came to getting that toaster oven secondhand.

The vinyl floor tiles were of a mixed variety as well, all leftovers from those same remodeling ventures. But her prized find was the old butcher's chopping-block stand that she used as a center island to ground the assorted eras she'd converged in the room. The island didn't sit level and the surface was beat all to hell and back, but still she cherished it.

She'd managed to replace all the broken windows in the house, again with castoffs from those moving to more energy-efficient choices. She'd painted the eighty-year-old wood siding herself. She'd painted the whole house as a matter of fact. Looking at it now made her proud even if she wasn't likely to be featured in *House Beautiful*.

The saloon was a similar project. The building and five acres she'd gotten for a song at a tax sell-off. Someone had abandoned the place and Laney had grabbed it, using her measly savings to purchase it flat-out and do the necessary renovations. She'd talked the president of a small local independent bank into taking a risk and lending her the money on her newly remodeled house so she could buy and renovate the saloon.

That had worked great at first. Problem was, she hadn't seen the nice older gentleman's bad side until it was too late. The loan had been on a balloon note which wasn't a problem at the time. Time flew and now that note came due in a mere ninety days. He had just informed her that he wouldn't be renewing the loan so the full amount was due in three months.

If she didn't pay, she would lose her business and her home. Worry crushed down on her shoulders.

Last month's receipts had looked stellar, and she had felt confident she had proof of steady-enough income to get a new loan elsewhere. But now the trouble with Terry and good workers walking had started a trend in falling revenue.

Many of her regulars were complaining that the guy made them uncomfortable. With all the wackos shooting up restaurants and the like, she could understand. But the last thing she needed was a drop in cash flow as the drop-dead date on getting a new loan approached.

She needed the books to look good. Laney choked back the anxiety and reminded herself that there was still time.

With the washing machine churning and the dishes done, she walked through the house to ensure the windows and doors were locked. Before Terry reappeared, she left her windows open at night during good weather. That was a risk she couldn't take with him lurking around. She couldn't trust him as far as she could throw him.

Keeping her .32 handy once Buddy was asleep was another new addition to her nightly routine. She hated that feeling of being afraid. She'd lived it too many times. Seemed just when life was looking up something else came along and rained on her parade.

She hesitated at the front window, one hand on the paper shade ready to drag it down. Her house sat a good fifty yards off the road and there were no streetlights on these old county roads, but the moon was big and bright tonight, giving her a clear view of the road that ran in front of her house.

A Jeep had parked on the shoulder directly in front of her house. With the convertible top removed, she could see that someone was behind the wheel but she couldn't begin to determine whether the driver was male or female. Definitely wasn't Terry's fancy import. Since his keys were at the High Noon, she could safely assume it wasn't him.

Unless he'd hitched or borrowed a ride from some jerk friend of his.

There was no logical reason for the driver to be stopped in front of her house unless he'd run out of gas. Since the closest convenience store was nearly all the way in town, a long ways from these twisting, winding roads, it wasn't smart to joyride out here without at least half a tank.

Evidently the guy didn't mind being seen since a few yards to the right or left of his position and her view would have been blocked by the trees in her yard. Not scary but definitely unsettling.

She didn't have any binoculars but she could get closer to have a better look and assess the situation. Knowing old man Kingston, he had a P.I. or member of his personal staff watching her, hoping she would make some sort of unfit-mother mistake. She had decided that making his old man happy was the only possible reason Terry was interested in Buddy after all this time. There had to be an agenda.

"Not happening, old man." He wasn't getting her son and she wasn't about to screw up. The thought that Kingston might be behind her banker's change of heart had crossed her mind. Failing to keep a roof over her son's head and food on the table might push her firmly into the unfit category.

"Don't borrow trouble, Laney."

She slid her cell into her back pocket and tucked the .32 in her waistband. She eased out the back door and made her way to the front of the house using the grapevine trellis and the old well house as cover. The trees and an abandoned tractor that was nearly as old as the house gave her a few points of cover from there. She'd considered having the old tractor hauled off when she first bought the place but she'd decided it gave the yard character. Her five acres had once been part of a huge family farm. It came with all sorts of funky character, like a leaky roof and unlevel floors.

The final tree available to shield her was only about ten yards from the road. She should be able to have a decent view of the interloper from there.

She rushed through the ankle-deep grass until she made her destination. Cutting the grass was something else she needed to find the time and energy to get done. Laney added the chore to her growing mental list.

Crouching behind the tree, she studied the vehicle and its driver. Male. The cowboy hat prevented her from making out his profile or his face.

As if he'd picked up on the thought, he removed his hat and placed it on the passenger seat. He leaned the seat back and appeared to be settling in for the night.

Strange.

He checked the screen of his cell phone and the glow highlighted his face.

Joel Hayden.

What the heck was he doing here?

Before her brain assimilated the best course of action, she pushed to her feet and strode toward him.

When he glanced her way, she demanded an answer. "What're you doing out here?"

He hopped out of the Jeep. The doors had been removed, leaving nothing between him and making that cocky move.

Her right hand rested on the butt of her Smith and Wesson. She kind of liked this guy, but the truth was he was a stranger and she had to be smart.

"I guess I should've knocked on the door and let you know I was here."

"I guess you should've." A frown nagged at her. "What're you doing?" How was it that her eyes couldn't stop surveying him from head to toe? The guy looked even better in the moonlight, but that was no excuse to go stupid.

He shrugged, set those big hands on his lean hips. "I was worried that guy might show up at your house after I kicked him out of the saloon."

Laney beat back the smile that tickled her lips. She did not know this man or his motives. As much as she wanted to be flattered by his chivalry, she couldn't ever be a fool again, especially when her son's safety was at stake. Still, she was flattered.

"That's very noble of you, Hayden, but your pay ends when you walk out the door of the High Noon."

"This isn't about getting paid overtime," he assured her.

"What's it about, then?" Her hand still rested on the weapon he could plainly see. "I warned you about those pickup lines. Persistence doesn't add any points."

"I have no patience for men like the one who gave you a hard time tonight," he explained in a firm tone that still reeked of charm. "Maybe I was a little rougher on him than I should have been. I don't want him taking out his frustration with me on you."

Wow, that really was sweet. "Nice of you to care, but honestly, you being out here now is kind of strange unless there's a hidden agenda. I don't know very many men—actually I don't know any—who would go so far out of their way just to be nice. So, what's the hitch?" Her cynicism was showing. That was never attractive.

He took a couple of steps toward her.

Her pulse reacted, but not in fear. She was attracted to this guy and that was dangerous.

You don't know him, Laney!

"I like you." He didn't stop until he was standing right in front of her in the grass that marked her property from the gravel road the state owned. "I don't have anything else to do and this felt like the right thing."

Before she could respond with something intelligent, he added, "I can leave if that's what you want."

"That'd probably be best."

She gave him her back and marched toward the house. In those few minutes in the moonlight she understood one very important thing about Hayden. He was trouble.

"Are you certain he won't come back?"

She hesitated. She shouldn't have. But he had a legitimate question.

Laney turned to face him. "He might but I doubt it."

He'd been damned drunk. Terry was probably sleeping it off at some dive motel with a honky-tonk honey who didn't have any better sense.

"Are you prepared to use that weapon if he does?"

That was none of his business. "If I have to."

"Do you know how to use it?"

No. "Of course. Why would I carry a weapon I can't use?"

"Because it makes you feel safe even when you have no idea how to use it."

Heat scorched her cheeks. "I said I know how to use it."

"You don't need to be afraid of me, Laney. I'm only here to help. No hidden agenda."

Okay, so maybe the guy was bored. As much

as she felt sure providing him with entertainment would be equally entertaining to her as well, that wasn't happening.

The last time she'd been in bed with a man was three years ago when she'd been stupid enough to believe more of Terry's lies. As much as she recognized her own needs—needs that she had ignored for far too long—she had a son to protect.

"Good night, Hayden."

"I'll be out of your way at sunup."

"Suit yourself."

To her amazement, she made it all the way to the house without looking back. A repeat of her nightly rounds in the house proved the doors and window were secure.

In her room, curtains and shades drawn, door closed, she stripped off her clothes. A shower would just have to wait until morning. She was way too tired. Besides, the washing machine was still running and that meant the water pressure in the shower would suck.

No, thanks.

She dragged on her favorite T-shirt, the one with that silly sponge character her son loved. Tucking her .32 on the shelf above her bed— way out of Buddy's reach even if he climbed up on the iron headboard—she realized she was sore from unloading that supply truck this afternoon.

She crawled into bed and her whole body sighed.

Her bed was the most awesome piece of furniture she owned besides the lumpy sofa.

Lying on her back, she stared at the slow turn of the ceiling fan blades in hopes that sleep would come quickly.

Didn't happen.

How could she hope to sleep with him out there watching?

Instead, her brain started throwing out scenarios that had nothing to do with a good working relationship with the cowboy.

Not smart, Laney.

The folks who liked her called her hardworking, nice, friendly…but not a one had ever accused her of being savvy when it came to spotting the devil behind a nice smile and good manners.

She had a feeling it was going to take her savviest maneuvers to head off this collision course.

Joel Hayden was going to be way, way more than she could handle.

Chapter Three

6:30 a.m.

The sun was up and the promise of an early summer scorcher was in the air.

Joel walked back toward his Jeep. The need to stretch his legs had awoken him before sunup. All remained quiet. The last of the lights had gone out in Laney's house around two. He doubted she and the boy would be up any time soon.

The past five nights had been spent like last night, only without Laney's knowledge. Parked out of her line of sight, Joel had slept in his Jeep—what sleep he'd gotten—in order to keep watch on her.

It wasn't the most comfortable assignment he'd had as far as getting any shut-eye but there was no way around it. For now, he couldn't ensure her safety via any other means.

Clare Barker was still unaccounted for. Her

whereabouts unknown since her great escape from the apartment in Copperas Cove. Rafe, her husband, remained on death row. His execution was barely more than three weeks away.

He'd been the one to contact the Colby Agency yet he'd shut down completely since learning of Clare's disappearance. In part, possibly, because he had learned the one person he had trusted and communicated with in recent years had double-crossed him by helping Clare elude the agency's surveillance.

Not a whole lot about this case made sense.

The necessity to keep the principals in the dark was primarily to ensure their safety. Until the Colby Agency discovered what Clare Barker was up to, these women's safety had to be top priority. If word got out, the media circus would hinder the agency's investigation. Disrupting the lives of the three women who had been confirmed as the long-missing Barker daughters was going to be problematic enough, mostly for them. Sadie Gilmore, the youngest, had accepted this new reality well enough, but there was no way to guess the reaction from the remaining two women. For now, keeping the investigation quiet and finding the truth as quickly as possible was essential.

Bottom line, it didn't have to make sense to

Joel or anyone else. His single mission was to protect Laney and her son.

He settled his Stetson in place and leaned against the front fender. A few more minutes and he would relocate to ensure Laney didn't grow any more suspicious than she already was.

Laney Seagers had no idea that she had been born Lisa Barker, middle daughter of Clare and Rafe Barker. Prints from her one arrest for assaulting the same jerk who was giving her a hard time at present had confirmed her identity. She had no idea and Joel wasn't looking forward to sharing that information. And he wouldn't until one of two things happened— the danger had passed or he was forced to do so in order to keep watch.

The lady seemed reasonably happy considering the less-than-kind hand fate had dealt her. Like most these days it was a rough go on the financial front, but she was managing or she had been until her banker decided to turn testy. To Laney, getting that loan taken care of was her biggest worry at the moment. She had no idea that far larger problems were brewing like dark clouds over her head.

Rafe and Clare Barker were two of Texas's most heinous criminals, the Princess Killers. The two had allegedly kidnapped and murdered more than a dozen young girls. That number didn't include their own daughters, who had disappeared under suspicious circumstances the morning of their arrests. The Barkers were sentenced to death. Though Clare's conviction had recently been overturned, according to her husband she was the one who had actually committed those gruesome murders more than twenty years ago.

Both had been arrested and charged, after so many young girls had gone missing in and around the community of Granger. Several bodies had been recovered from the Barker property. But the bodies of some of the missing as well as those of their three little daughters had not been found.

Now Joel and the other folks at the Colby Agency knew the reason why. Rafe Barker claimed he had turned the girls over to a trusted friend to ensure their safety from their crazy mother. To that end, he'd staged the family car and their room to make it look as if he'd killed them. But now that Clare's conviction had been overturned, he feared for their lives.

The Colby Agency had no idea as of yet if there was any validity to Rafe's claim of innocence, but he had been right about his daughters. The woman, Janet Tolliver, he had alleged was his accomplice in that eleventh-hour move to protect his girls had, in fact, arranged for their private, off-the-record adoptions.

Regrettably, she had been murdered within twenty-four hours of Clare's release. So far there was no proof Clare had anything to do with the murder, but they now knew that Clare had an accomplice. A one-armed man by the name of Tony Weeden.

As an infirmary nurse, Weeden had befriended Rafe Barker. Weeden was the one person to whom Rafe had told his story—until Rafe contacted the Colby Agency. His letter to Victoria Colby-Camp had been smuggled from Polunsky Prison by Weeden.

Whatever scheme was in motion and whoever was telling the truth, there was damned good reason to believe the Barker girls were in danger. The only question was from whom.

Sadie Gilmore, born Sarah Barker and the youngest of the three, was already in the capable hands of Colby investigator Lyle McCaleb.

Russ St. James had his eye on the unpredictable Olivia Westfield, born Olivia Barker, the oldest of the three. When reviewing the background files on the Barker girls, Joel had expected that his assignment would prove the most troublesome. Laney Seagers had a record of violence, though not exactly a rap sheet as long as her arm. She'd been in and out of one kind of trouble or another during her teenage years. She was also the only one of the three sisters with a kid in tow.

So far the biggest issue was with her ex-boyfriend and the father of her child. Still, Joel hadn't attempted to move in close to his mark until last night. He supposed the next couple of days would reveal a clearer picture of what lay ahead as far as his ability to gain her trust.

As if his thoughts had summoned her, Laney stepped out onto her front porch, settled her attention directly on him and headed his way.

He'd promised to be gone by sunup. Maybe he'd lingered too long. Laney seemed to appreciate his charm to a point, but she was far too wise of the ways of men to be fooled for long. She had no intention of falling into a trap of any sort. The lady was definitely jaded when it came to all things male. But she was attracted to him.

Jeans skintight, T-shirt just as formfitting, she strode purposefully toward him. Her hair bounced around her shoulders, the gold catching the early morning sun and shining like silk.

Now that would be a hell of a vision to wake up to every morning for the rest of a guy's life. Even a hardcore bachelor like him could appreciate that prospect.

"You're up early." He smiled, gave her a nod.

"Saw you walking around out here at the crack of dawn yourself." She set her hands on her hips and looked him up and down. "I imagine you could use a cup of coffee before you go back to town." She shrugged. "It's the least I can do after you stood guard all night."

He cast a speculative glance at the waist of her jeans. "Decided you didn't need your weapon this morning?"

She smiled. Not one of those full-blown make-his-heart-thump kind but sexy as hell nonetheless. "I'm a little paranoid at night. Afraid of the dark as a kid. You know how it goes. Some of us just don't grow out of it."

"Never had any trouble in the dark." He matched her smile. "But I have my moments with paranoia."

"So, you interested in coffee? I grind the beans every morning."

"Hard to refuse an offer like that."

"Is that a yes, Mr. Hayden?"

"Hop in." He grinned. "Considering the miles you walk most nights from one end of that bar to the other, taking a load off won't hurt." Not that he minded watching her walk.

"That's a nice Jeep." She climbed into the passenger seat. "Looks new."

"It's a couple years old." He cranked the engine. "Bought it for my thirty-second birthday. I guess it's my midlife-crisis car."

"At least you didn't get a massive truck." She shook her head as he rolled along her dirt driveway. "Some guys think they either have to buy the biggest truck or the fastest car. For some crazy reason they think it's a chick magnet."

He glanced at her as he parked in front of her house. "You mean it's not?"

"Definitely not." She admired the interior of his Jeep. "A vehicle should suit the man and his purpose in life."

"Never really thought about it that way."

Her gaze settled on his. "What's your purpose, Hayden? You got a house? A wife? Kids?"

He laughed. "No. No. And, no. Did I pass the test?"

She swung her legs to her right and hopped to the ground. "I haven't decided yet."

He wondered what her old beat-up Chevy said about her purpose. Just getting by? Or laid-back and happy to go with the flow?

"I know what you're thinking." She strode up onto the porch.

If she was a mind reader they were in serious trouble. "Is that right?"

She nodded. "You're wondering why I drive that old truck."

He pushed up his hat and studied her a moment. "The thought has crossed my mind." He wouldn't mention how recently.

"It was my father's." She turned toward the old blue vehicle. "It was the only thing left after the fire. A buddy of my dad's saved it for me. Took him a while to find me with the bouncing around from one foster home to the other. It's a damn good vehicle. Since I was sixteen it's been the one reliable thing in my life. Got me where I needed to go. Even served as a home sometimes."

"That beats the hell out of a high-tech sound system and power windows any day of the week."

"Damn straight."

The screen door whined as she swung it open. The old house had a comfortable feel about it. Swing on the front porch. Pot of colorful flowers near the door. Old-fashioned screen door fronting an even older slab door with glass so old it had that wavy look. Inside, the place was well-kept and smelled of fresh-brewed coffee.

Likely every part of the decorating and furnishings were secondhand but she'd done a nice job making the place feel like a home for her and the boy.

"Buddy still asleep?" Joel didn't have a doubt that if the kid was conscious he would be either following his mom around or designing the next rocket for space exploration. As smart as he was, he didn't appear to have any playmates his age. The kid didn't seem to mind.

"He'll be up soon and then he won't slow down until he crashes for the night."

Joel laughed. "Kids that age never slow down unless they're sick."

"Thought you didn't have any kids."

The remark was tossed offhandedly enough but Joel suspected it was one of those self-protective measures. "Lots of nieces and nephews."

In the kitchen, there was more of Laney's eclectic decorating. Again, lots of repurposed items. He was impressed with her ingenuity. A lot of things about the lady impressed him. She grabbed a mug from the rack and poured the coffee.

"Smells good." He accepted the cup and savored a long swallow. "Hmm. You have a special blend?"

She patted a glass container. "I mix a few different beans to get the perfect combination of light and dark, French and Colombian. It's the best mix I've come up with so far." She wrinkled her nose. "Sounds kind of tragic but it's a hobby of mine."

Judging by the large pot rack hanging over her island and the broad selection of cooking implements, the lady liked to cook. "Did you do the decorating yourself?"

She cradled a mug of her special brew in both hands. "I did. The remodeling and the decorating. I spent a lot of time in salvage stores and hustling to remodeling sales. It got to be a kind of competition with myself to see how much money I could save."

"Looks like you have a knack."

"That's what my grandmother said." She smiled, remembering. "I was just a kid when I helped her remodel her old farmhouse. She was all by herself and my parents were on the road with business all the time. One day we just tore into the place and started fixing things up. It was a learning experience, let me tell you."

"Your folks live around here?"

She shook her head. "They're all long gone. Died when I was a kid. Had foster parents through my crazy teenage years and, believe it or not, I just got a little crazier after that. I didn't get my act together until I had Buddy."

He knew her history but asking the logical questions was necessary for his cover. "Well, you turned out pretty damned good, Ms. Seagers."

Those brown eyes searched his. "What's a guy like you doing hanging around the High Noon and tossing out compliments to lonely women?" She heaved one shoulder then let it fall. "Or here, for that matter? You're clearly educated, polished. Not the usual cowboy who hangs out in saloons."

"The company I worked for went south. I have some savings. I decided taking a little time off to just chill would be a good thing."

"You seem a little young to retire."

He laughed. "True. But there's a high burnout rate in security services. A lot of pressure and a lot of long days and even longer weeks."

"You're on break," she suggested, her expression a bit wary and openly disappointed.

He nodded. "I guess I am."

"Why bother with working for me? I mean, it's still security work. Last night can't be your idea of chilling."

"Definitely not the same." He finished off his coffee. "Most of my work involved high-risk principals. Politicians, celebrities. Lot of pressure. Last night was a cakewalk."

She poured him another cup. "You meet anybody really famous?"

"You mean like a rock star or movie star?" he teased.

She scooted up onto the counter. "Yeah, that's exactly what I mean."

"A few. A former president and vice president impressed me the most."

"Wow." She pursed her lips. "I may have to get you a special T-shirt for work."

"Does that mean I have the job?"

She held his gaze for a bit. He didn't miss the hesitation in her eyes. "I don't usually trust people right off the bat. I take a while, most of the time. But for some reason I do trust you, Hayden."

That should have made him relax. It sure would make his assignment a hell of a lot easier. But it also meant that she would eventually learn that he wasn't telling her the whole truth. Knowing that she had decided to trust him made that part a whole lot harder.

"I'm flattered," he confessed. A woman like her didn't trust easily.

"Just make sure you don't make me regret it. And when you're ready to go back to your real life, I expect a two-week notice."

The tension held a moment. "You have my word."

Another second or two of that thick silence elapsed.

"I guess you have the job, then. Barring any unflattering information from your references."

"Fair enough." He narrowed his gaze at her. "Now I have a question for you."

Her expression turned skeptical. "Be aware, I reserve the right not to answer."

"Agreed."

"So ask."

"Why're you lonely?"

She looked confused.

Before she could put two and two together, he went on with the question that had nothing to do with his assignment. "A woman as young, smart and hot as you should never be lonely."

Surprise flashed in her eyes but quickly reverted to wariness. "I was trying to be funny, Hayden. I don't have time to be lonely."

He'd hit a nerve there. He glanced at the array of hanging pots and pans. "You must be a heck of a chef."

"I can hold my own." She set her cup aside, visibly relaxed. "The only time I've ever known a man to be interested in kitchen utensils was if he was a chef himself or if he was hungry."

Joel grinned. "I'm afraid my culinary skills leave something to be desired."

Laney folded her arms across her chest. "I'll make a deal with you, Hayden. You cut the grass and I'll make you a breakfast you'll tell your grandkids about."

"Deal."

Joel was only too glad to help.

One step closer to where he needed to be.

Chapter Four

Victoria Colby-Camp reviewed the records they had amassed on the Barker case. What was she missing?

Each step taken by the investigating detectives after the arrest of the Barkers was spot-on. There was every reason to believe that the Barker girls had died that final morning before their parents' arrests. The blood at the house and in the family car had suggested foul play. The blood type was consistent with that of the little girls. The bodies were not recovered and no trace of the girls had been discovered in all these years.

Until now.

If Janet Tolliver, Rafe Barker's friend who had helped with whisking away the children, had lived, perhaps she would have been willing to cooperate with the agency's investigation and solved at least part of this mystery.

But she had been murdered and the killer was still out there. Had she been killed by another of Rafe's confidants? That wasn't logical and no other resource he might have used had been discovered.

And why would he kill the woman who had kept his secret all these years? To cover his tracks? Had Janet Tolliver known incriminating information beyond the location of the three Barker daughters?

If Rafe hadn't orchestrated her murder, had Clare? Not likely. Lucas, Victoria's husband, had been keeping watch on Clare until she vanished with Tony Weeden, the one-armed man. There simply had been no real opportunity for Clare to have gotten to Janet. Unless Weeden had committed the act for her or for Rafe.

Weeden was the only variable. It had to be him. For one thing, he was left-handed, out of necessity, but a leftie nonetheless. The police in Copperas Cove had determined that the blow that ultimately killed Janet Tolliver had likely been wielded by a person who was left-handed. The murder weapon was thought to have been a heavy marble angel statue from Janet's home. The killer had obviously taken the time to clean it thoroughly as well as anything else he or she may have touched in the home. But trace amounts of Janet's blood had been found on the statue. Since the statue hadn't been lying near her body, the blood hadn't simply splattered there.

But if Rafe hadn't ordered Janet's murder, which his doing so would have made no sense, why had Weeden turned on Rafe and murdered the woman who had ensured the safety of Rafe's daughters? That scenario made no sense, either. But someone had murdered her and that murderer had a motive. Had Weeden been waiting for just the right opportunity to take vengeance on Rafe or Janet?

For what reason?

Was Weeden somehow connected to Clare beyond the role of accomplice? If so, why had they not found a connection in his history? Weeden was raised by foster parents but his birth record was ambiguous to say the least. Simon Ruhl, the head of the Colby West offices, was convinced the record was a forgery.

So many questions and hardly any answers.

Victoria heaved a weary sigh. The day had scarcely begun and already she felt emotionally drained.

Time was short and all at the Houston Colby office were working overtime to solve this complex puzzle, including Victoria and Lucas.

The idea of an innocent man being put to death twisted her insides. But was there time enough to prove who was innocent and who was guilty?

Victoria thought of the way Rafe had looked at her when she revealed that Weeden had deceived him. The devastation had been clear in his eyes but it was the other emotion—something like rage—that disturbed her immensely. Forced her to rethink his motives and his story.

Was she working with the devil himself?

A rap at the door drew Victoria from the troubling thoughts. Simon and Lucas entered the small conference room where, together with Victoria, they had created a timeline of events along a whiteboard that extended across the better part of one wall. Photos, newspaper clippings, it was all there.

"We have a new development that may prove our first real break in the case," Simon announced as he and Lucas joined Victoria at the conference table.

"We could certainly use one." Though they had uncovered small details over the course of the past few days, not one had propelled the investigation forward.

"As you know," Lucas began, his expression cautiously optimistic, "I've spent the past forty-eight hours attempting to track down anyone who knew either Clare or Rafe in college, before their marriage."

Anticipation trickled in Victoria's veins. Lucas had that look in his eyes. He'd found something. "And?"

"A Francine Parks was a close friend of Clare's for the first year they attended the same university. She claims Clare was raped by one of their professors but she refused to report the incident for fear that the scandal would somehow cause the loss of her scholarship. This woman believes a pregnancy resulted from the rape."

"This would have been thirty-one or thirty-two years ago?" Clare was about the same age as Victoria.

"Thirty-two," Lucas confirmed.

Simon picked up where Lucas had left off. "Ms. Parks is certain Clare gave birth to a child conceived in the assault. But she has no proof. She is basing her assumption on excessive weight gain and repeated bouts of something like morning sickness those final few weeks of the spring semester. The following fall, Clare returned looking and behaving as if nothing had happened. According to Parks she refused to discuss the incident at any time."

"But this Francine Parks can't be sure," Victoria guessed.

"She cannot," Simon confirmed.

It was definitely a possible lead, though not a particularly reliable one. Hearsay was just that, hearsay.

"According to Parks," Lucas noted, "the incident occurred in late November which would suggest a July or August delivery date. The timing could imply that perhaps Tony Weeden is Clare's son and, frankly, I'm inclined to believe the Parks woman. She has no horse in this race."

"The age would be right." Victoria resisted jumping to the immediate conclusion. "Did Ms. Parks have any other reason to believe that a child resulted from the attack? An overheard conversation? Rumors around the campus?"

"None," Simon answered. "Clare requested a different roommate that fall and apparently kept to herself since we haven't been able to find anyone she was close to until she met Rafe." Simon sat back in his chair and seemed to consider the possibilities. "Clare was young, only twenty-one. Her parents, the Sneads, were murdered when she was a kid. At eighteen, she left her foster parents without looking back. But," he countered, "she did have a sister, Janet Tolliver. Might she have turned to her? That would provide the connection between the three."

"You're assuming," Victoria suggested, "that Clare knew where her biological sister ended up."

"We've learned the Tollivers, the people who raised Janet, and the Sneads, Clare's parents, were friends," Simon reminded her. "Our thinking when we first discovered that Janet and Clare were biological sisters was that the Sneads gave Janet up due to financial reasons but that may not have been the case. The one source we found who knew the Tolliver family at the time Janet came to live with them suggested the Sneads had been afraid of Janet. There was talk that she tried repeatedly to harm her younger sister, Clare, and that was the reason for the Sneads sending Janet away."

"Is this source that reliable?" Victoria was sure both Lucas and Simon understood that accuracy was key not only for finding the truth but also for moving forward in the proper direction. "We have little time, gentlemen, for running theories that prove groundless. We need something solid. And we need it now."

Lucas joined the conversation. "The woman who lived next door to the Tolliver family is old, and her memory is sketchy on some aspects of how Janet came to be a part of the Tolliver family, but she was absolutely certain of that point. The Tollivers had no other children at home. They were all grown, so they never saw any trouble out of Janet. She gave the appearance of a nice young girl but the neighbor was not comfortable around her."

"We're checking with old schoolmates and any living teachers," Simon explained, "to determine if Janet had any problems at school."

"We learned nothing else from Janet's neighbor in Copperas Cove who held the photo albums of Rafe's daughters for her?"

Simon shook his head. "The neighbor knew the aunt who left the house to Janet. She and Janet saw each other occasionally as children but their friendship was more recent and, I suspect, relatively superficial."

Were they wasting their time digging up information on a dead woman? Maybe, but they simply had no other leads. There was nowhere else to go in light of Rafe Barker's abrupt silence.

"Would Clare turn to a sister who had tried to harm her as a child?" Seemed a more than reasonable question to Victoria. Victoria had a younger sister of her own who had proven that blood was not always thicker than water.

What exactly had happened to tear apart Clare's family and to set her on a course to connect with Rafe Barker? Had he turned her evil or had she changed him?

"Clare may not have known about the incident or perhaps didn't comprehend the magnitude of what actually happened." Simon had children of his own and would certainly understand the capacity of young ones for forgiveness. "She was three when Janet was sent away. Her parents may have chosen not to tell her or she may have simply blocked the incidents from her memory."

"Then again, Janet may have sought out Clare." Victoria understood the need to find long-lost loved ones. "She was certainly old enough to remember a sister even if she chose not to remember certain events." Then again, the prison logs listed no visitor named Janet Tolliver for Clare or for Rafe.

"Janet may have done more than that," Lucas interjected. "After Clare's parents were murdered, a couple of neighbors stated they saw a teenage girl outside the home. The lead proved a dead end. But what if it was Janet? What if she came back—she would have been fourteen at the time—and killed the parents who deserted her? Perhaps she even hoped it would be blamed on Clare as punishment for being the daughter they kept."

"Then why would Clare see Janet again? Even after being raped and feeling utterly alone?" That part didn't feel right to Victoria. The police reports from the time Clare's parents were murdered indicated that she had come home and found the tragedy. Yet she had been covered in blood. From her attempts to save them, she had claimed.

So much death and devastation. Would this tragic cycle end with the surviving Barker daughters? Victoria intended to ensure the nightmare ended with this investigation.

"Clare may have blocked the horror of that evening from her mind, as well," Lucas offered. "It's far easier to fall back into a pattern that worked once than to stand up and face such a terrible truth."

Her husband had a very good point. Victoria had long thought that the tragedy of her own son's abduction and the twenty years they had lost was the worst a woman and mother could suffer. This frightening family saga had her rethinking the definition of "worst-case scenario."

"If the two were in contact again," Simon proposed, "Janet may have taken care of the child born to Clare just as she did her three daughters years later."

But Janet Tolliver had taken the three girls for Rafe, not for Clare.

"That possibility, however, gives Clare less of a motive for murdering Janet," Victoria suggested. "Why kill the person who helped her with such a tremendous burden at a critical time in her life?"

"Because she discovered that Janet had hidden her daughters from her…and then refused to tell her once she was released where they are," Simon offered.

"Janet had even gone so far as to hide the photo albums she had saved," Lucas pointed out. "With the woman next door. Seems to me she wanted to make sure Clare didn't get her hands on them."

The photo albums. All three were well-documented biographies of the girls' lives, from their original birth certificates to current photos. All apparently recorded by Janet Tolliver.

"Assuming Weeden is, in fact, Clare's son, he may have killed Janet in an effort to help his mother," Simon summed up. "The flip side of that is that possibly Weeden is only pretending to help his mother. He may have an entirely different motive and agenda."

"Revenge," Lucas agreed. "He was the child his mother abandoned. Subsequently marrying and having three little girls."

More theories and scenarios and no answers, Victoria thought. She banished the mounting worries. "Where are we on Laney and Olivia?"

"Hayden called in this morning," Simon reported. "He's making good progress. St. James is still watching Olivia from a distance."

"Both are very good at what they do," Lucas tacked on. "Laney and Olivia are in good hands, even from a distance."

Victoria prayed they could keep these women safe.

And she hoped solving this puzzle would not be too late to stop an innocent man from being executed.

If he was indeed innocent.

Chapter Five

Laney leaned in the open doorway to watch what she typically considered a boring task. But with Hayden pushing that lawn mower, his shirt long ago tossed aside, she had to confess there was absolutely nothing boring about the view. Broad shoulders, lean waist with those ripped abs… Very nice.

That little voice that always reminded her of how often she'd been an idiot tried to intrude but she ignored it. Hayden had no idea she was watching and she deserved a little stolen pleasure here and there.

Lonely. Yes, she was lonely. No use lying to herself. But she had no time to quench that particular thirst.

Couldn't hurt to look. It was the touching that led to trouble.

In the living room behind her, Buddy watched

his one hour of television. The restriction wasn't one she had enforced; it was his own. He had two thirty-minute programs he considered his must-watch TV then he was done. On to one of his games or to his Lego corner to design and build something new. Having such a bright kid was intimidating at times. No matter the cost to her personally, she wanted him to have every opportunity in life.

As for Laney, she could be happy just to daydream. Her attention wandered back to the man finishing up the nice job in her yard. She couldn't remember the last time anyone had done a menial chore for her. In part because she was so independent she rarely allowed anyone to know she needed help. But mostly because she'd always picked the wrong kind of guys. The ones not at all interested in helping with anything other than separating her from her panties.

At twenty-six it was darned well past time she'd recognized her destructive pattern and changed course. Her gaze tracked Hayden a moment longer. Falling back into bad habits was a bad idea. The next man she allowed herself to get involved with would earn the right to be with her.

A good-looking cowboy on break from his life wasn't the right starting place.

The smell of biscuits browning in the oven tickled her nose and reminded her that the only promise she'd made to her new sexy security guy was breakfast.

After a quick check on Buddy, she headed back to the kitchen. Eggs and bacon were staying warm in the covered cast-iron skillet. She grabbed an oven mitt and peeked in on the biscuits.

"Perfect." And homemade. That was another thing her grandmother had taught her. How to make super-fluffy biscuits. One of these days she intended to start opening the saloon for breakfast. Experimenting with coffee was a fun hobby that had her hankering to take it to the next level. The interstate passed right by the saloon. She was far enough out of Beaumont proper to make going for breakfast from that end of the city limits a pain. Why not capitalize on the convenient location?

The roar of the mower stopped. Laney glanced out the window just in time to see Hayden drag his T-shirt back over his head. If her stomach weren't rioting with hunger pangs from the smell of the biscuits she'd swear it was gawking at him that was tightening her insides.

She grabbed a strip of crisp bacon and tore off a bite. "You're just hungry, girl. And not for him."

With her mismatched stoneware on the kitchen table and a fresh pot of coffee filling the room with its robust aroma, she smiled as he strolled in through the back door.

"My yard looks more like a lawn now than the makings of a hay field. Thanks." Fact was, she couldn't remember when the lawn had looked so well manicured.

"I'm the one who should be thanking you." He rubbed his flat belly. "Breakfast smells fantastic."

Oh, yeah. The man was a bachelor all right. Otherwise plain old morning staples wouldn't have him tossing around words like *fantastic*.

"Nothing you couldn't get at any old breakfast hut."

He raised his eyebrows at the platter of biscuits. "I'm reasonably confident you're wrong about that."

"Bathroom's down the hall. Wash up and I'll serve."

"Whatever you say, boss lady." He winked and strode off to follow her order.

Laney shook her head. No one should fit that well into a pair of jeans. Or look that good all sweaty and smelling like fresh-cut grass.

Buddy wandered over and leaned against her leg. "Does he live here now, Mommy?"

"Of course not. This is our house. We live

here. Just you and me." Laney lifted her munchkin into her arms and gave him a hug. "Wow, you're getting almost too big for me to pick up, young man."

He pressed his nose to hers. "Biscuits. I need more energy for the town I'm buildin'."

She grinned. "Biscuits will do it." Laney settled him on the floor. "Pick your seat." He never chose the same chair twice in a row.

"Purple feet!" He slid into the one on the far end of the table.

"That's the best one." Same thing she told him every time no matter which chair he selected.

Like the rest of her furniture, her table and chairs were mismatched. She'd decided to throw a little excitement into mealtime so she'd given each chair a personality by painting each a different color with faces and painted-on hair. She'd even attached small wooden shapes to the legs and painted each as a foot or a shoe. She might have gone a little overboard with the beads and bow ties on the backs of the chairs but Buddy loved them.

The air changed in the room when Hayden returned. Maybe it was the breeze from the window. The chill bumps on her skin certainly weren't the result of him simply entering the room.

"Good morning, Buddy."

"You have to sit down there." Buddy pointed to the other end of the table. "That's for company."

"Sounds like the best seat in the house. Definitely the chair with the best feet."

Laney threw off her apron and joined them at the table. "Actually it's the one with an uneven leg." She arrowed a look at her son. "I'll take that one."

Hayden pulled out the chair. "Love the feet."

Laney settled in the chair, and it immediately tilted a smidge to one side. "I got the idea from a magazine."

He took the seat to her left. "You have a very artistic flare and a vivid imagination."

"I'll take that as a compliment."

"That was the point." Hayden sent her another of those unabashed winks.

Laney focused on the food. Buddy had already filled his plate with far more than he could possibly eat. Laney loaded Hayden's and then her own. She was starving.

At the same time, he poured the coffee, their movements choreographed as smoothly as if they shared breakfast every day.

She speared a clump of scrambled eggs. What the heck was wrong with her? Evidently the financial worries and frustration with Terry were messing with her brain.

"You looking forward to school this fall?" Hayden asked her son.

Buddy looked up, a biscuit halfway to his mouth. "I'm not sure yet."

That was her boy. "You liked it when we went for that orientation visit a couple weeks ago."

He chewed off a big bite of biscuit and shrugged.

"He's a little worried that he won't fit in," Laney explained. "He doesn't know any of the other kids who'll be starting with him."

"Sounds like you need to join one of the ball teams," Hayden said to Buddy. "I've seen flyers all over town about sign-ups."

Buddy turned up his glass of milk then pursed his lips while he considered the suggestion. "I'm not really T-ball material. I prob'ly couldn't hit the ball and then I'd get bored."

Hayden nodded. "Yeah, that would be kind of boring."

Laney focused on her plate and hoped the men wouldn't notice the laughter she was barely restraining.

"'Course," Hayden went on, "a man puts a little practice into it, he could probably hit that ball every single time."

"I don't have a ball or a bat," Buddy explained. "That makes practicing a problem."

"I'm sure we can do something about that." Hayden glanced at Laney before he turned back to the boy. "I made all-star every year in high school. I could give you a few pointers."

Buddy's face furrowed in concentration. "That was a long time ago. You might be rusty."

Laney couldn't help herself; she laughed. She tried to cover her mouth but there was no holding it back.

Hayden nodded, managed to keep a straight face somehow. "How about I get the gear we need and we practice together?"

Another fierce moment of concentration puckered her little boy's face. "We'll see."

"Good deal." Hayden glanced at her again, amusement shining in his eyes.

Laney wanted to smile at the idea but would Hayden really stick around long enough to keep that promise?

The screen door whined, announcing someone was at the front door before the firm knock echoed.

"Excuse me, gentlemen." She flashed a smile at Hayden. Maybe he wouldn't break her boy's heart...or hers.

As much as her son's vocabulary and intelligence thrilled Laney she did worry about him fitting in at school. She sighed. That was one worry she couldn't do anything about right now.

Laney opened the door expecting to have to kick Terry off her porch or to see the mailman dropping off a package. But the man waiting on her porch was a stranger. He wore a suit and tie, glasses and sported a slicked-down comb-over. He carried a black leather briefcase, the thin kind that was useless for anything other than a few papers.

"Ms. Seagers?"

Apprehension needled its way under her skin. "That's me."

"I'm Howard Samson from Samson and Lott Appraisers. Mr. Teague from Beaumont Independent Bank commissioned me to execute an appraisal of your property."

What the...? "I'm afraid you have me at a disadvantage, Mr. Samson. I wasn't aware an appraisal had been ordered." The apprehension swelled into downright fear.

"I assure you, Ms. Seagers, it's standard procedure when a loan nears maturity and the refinancing is questionable."

Standard procedure. Old man Teague just couldn't wait to assess the value of her property. Damn him and damn Kingston if he had anything to do with it.

"We're in the middle of having breakfast." She was angry now. How dare that old goat do this? "Maybe you could call for an appointment next time."

"I understand," he offered in that monotone that matched his neutral expression. "I'll be taking measurements and photos outside first. When you're ready for me to come inside you can let me know."

"The lady said you needed an appointment."

Laney's breath caught at the warning in Hayden's voice. He'd moved in right behind her and she hadn't even noticed.

Samson's eyebrows reared up his forehead. "I see."

"Good," Hayden offered. "You have a good day now." He closed the door in the guy's face.

Laney stared at him. She wasn't sure whether to kick him or to hug him.

"Sorry," he muttered irreverently. "I have no patience for jerks and that guy was a jerk."

Heat singed her cheeks. She walked past him to check on Buddy. He'd finished and was busy piling his dishes into the sudsy water now filling the old porcelain sink, egg and biscuit remains going for a swim.

She turned back to Hayden. "I guess you've

heard the rumors about my impending loan crisis." Her staff had a bad habit of eavesdropping.

"I did," he admitted.

She blew out a breath of frustration. "It's not pretty but I'm not giving up."

"Giving up is for wimps." He gave her a reassuring smile that felt more reassuring than it should have.

This man was almost as much a stranger as the one who'd just showed up at her door.

"Thanks for the breakfast. I'll stow the mower." He ran a hand through his hair. She shivered. "I noticed the barn needs a few repairs to the roof. Unless my boss tells me different, I'm free all day to work on that."

Laney ignored the floor shifting beneath her feet. This was too much. It wasn't that she didn't appreciate the help and he'd been really nice to her son...but this was a risk she wasn't prepared to take.

"You're a really nice guy and all," she said, searching for a kind way to say what needed to be said.

He held up both hands. "I get it. You don't trust me."

Wow. Hearing him say it sounded a lot worse than she'd been aiming for. "I guess that's what I'm trying to say."

"I get it. Really." He set his hands on his hips. "Call my references. You'll feel better then."

"You're right. Sure." She slid her fingers into her front pockets. "I'm sorry but my son is my top priority and as much…"

Stop, Laney. That was enough. She didn't have to explain herself. This was the right thing to do. He would either understand or he wouldn't.

"I'll see you tonight at the High Noon."

She nodded. "Thank you for…helping out."

He patted that amazing six-pack. "Thanks for the home-cooked meal. It's been a while."

"Mom!"

Laney pushed aside the mixed feelings she couldn't seem to shake. "What you got, sweetie?"

He held up one of his latest art endeavors she'd had hanging on the fridge. "This one is extra good."

Laney crouched down to his eye level. "It sure is." He'd drawn a picture of the two of them flying a kite. This was his first year to be able to hang on to the kite string all by himself.

"Can I give it to the lady?"

Laney frowned. "What lady?"

Buddy looked at her as if she should know

exactly who he meant. "The grandma lady who played with me in the kitchen last night."

Fear ignited deep in Laney's gut. "What grandma lady?"

Buddy huffed. "The one who washed dishes for Uncle Tater."

Laney relaxed. "A friend of Tater's?"

Buddy shrugged. "I don't know. She was nice. I wanna give her this."

Hayden crouched down next to Laney. "Is this lady your uncle Tater's grandmother?" he asked Buddy.

Laney frowned. "He doesn't have any relatives in Texas."

Buddy eased closer to his mother and shrugged again.

"I guess it'd be okay to give her the drawing." Laney hugged her son. "That's very sweet of you."

Buddy wiggled out of her arms and smiled. "She'll like it."

"How do you know the lady was a grandmother?" Hayden asked.

What was with all the questions? she wondered. Before she could ask that very question, Buddy answered. "She had grandma hair."

"Gray hair?" he prompted.

Buddy nodded. "That means she's old."

"Was her hair long like your mother's?" He tugged on a lock of Laney's hair.

With a big shake of his head, Buddy touched her chin. "Short like there."

"Did she ask you any questions, little man?"

Buddy frowned. "I'm not a man. I'm a little boy." He turned to Laney. "Tell him, Mom. He's confused."

Laney searched Hayden's eyes. "You heard him. You need to see his driver's license to confirm his age?"

"Mommy." Buddy made a face. "That's silly."

"Did this nice grandmother ask you any questions about you and your mom?" Hayden rephrased his question.

"Nope. She asked me about Mr. Bear."

Hayden swung his attention to Laney. "Mr. Bear?"

"Why don't you introduce Mr. Bear to Mr. Hayden?"

"Okay." Buddy hustled off to his bedroom.

Laney pushed to her feet. "Why all the questions? I'm sure the lady was a friend of Tatum's. He has friends stop by and hang out with him in the kitchen occasionally."

Hayden stood. "I saw something on the news before I left Houston about an older woman involved with a human-trafficking ring that deals in young children."

The very idea made Laney's chest hurt. She rubbed at the tightness there. "Are you serious?"

"Afraid so."

"Jesus. I'll have to talk to Tatum."

"You should ask him to keep the kitchen door locked."

That barb of fear twisted a little tighter inside her. "Absolutely."

Buddy shuffled back into the room, Mr. Bear hugged to his chest. He glanced shyly at Hayden.

He crouched down and pretended to shake the bear's hand. "Nice to meet you, Mr. Bear."

Buddy smiled, something he rarely did with strangers. "The grandma lady said her daughter had a teddy bear just like him."

The notion that this woman could be the one in the news report Hayden mentioned seemed like a long shot. She was probably just one of Tater's friends. A silly coincidence.

But the sudden grim expression on Hayden's face sent a chill straight through her.

As protective as she was of her son, surely she hadn't been totally oblivious to that kind of danger walking right into her own saloon.

But then she'd been overwhelmed lately.

Had Buddy's safety suffered because of her inability to handle the stress load right now?

Laney chased away the worries. It wouldn't happen again. She would see to that.

Chapter Six

Noon

When Tatum Motley, aka Uncle Tater, arrived half an hour ago, Joel had given him and Laney some space. Though she hadn't said as much out loud, she had clearly wanted to talk to her employee and friend privately.

Joel understood her situation. As much as she would prefer to have her son at her side at all times, she had to run the bar—which meant Buddy had to be in the kitchen or the office away from the dispensing and selling of liquor. Laney trusted the retired sailor but she would need to get it through his head that extreme caution was necessary from this point forward.

Laney had suggested maybe Kingston had sent the old lady to freak her out or to prove Buddy wasn't safe at the High Noon.

She just didn't know.

Joel offered to keep an eye on Buddy while

he played in the backyard. It gave Joel a chance to call the agency with this latest development. Simon Ruhl agreed that despite the lack of proof that the grandmotherly woman, as Buddy had described, was in fact Clare Barker, there was every reason to suspect she was here and, at the very least, watching.

Lucas Camp, Victoria's husband, and a former CIA agent, was en route. Clare Barker had given him the slip in Copperas Cove a few days ago. Lucas had been attempting to pick up her trail again since. He would be nearby and available if Joel needed backup.

Hopefully it wouldn't come to that but better to be safe than sorry. This was a highly sensitive situation with charged emotions for all involved.

At this point Joel would have no choice but to add the next layer to his cover profile. As much as he disliked lying to the lady, it was, unfortunately, necessary to ensure she didn't grow suspicious of his interest in this mysterious visitor.

Leaning against the post nearest the steps on the back porch, he watched Buddy climb the ladder to the slide, then squeal as he slid down. The kid was cute and so damned smart. But he was still just a kid and had no concept of the danger associated with talking to a stranger. The kid needed playtime with others his own age.

Joel had no real experience with kids but that requirement seemed logical to him. If he bothered to say as much, Laney would likely put him in his place. The woman was seriously protective of her son and defensive of her mothering skills. He supposed dealing with a sleaze like Terry Kingston had generated that touchy situation.

Buddy hopped into a swing seat and struggled to get the thing going. The seat needed to be lowered a bit. Joel could handle that.

He strolled over and propped against the slide ladder. Like his mother, the boy had a strong sense of independence. Approaching the suggestion from the wrong perspective would offend the little fellow.

"When I was your age," Joel commented, "I liked to be able to push off with my feet."

Buddy started grunting and wrestling with the momentum and stared at the ground a good six inches below his boots. "I'll have to grow some more before I can do that."

"Guess so." Joel pushed his hat up a notch. "Unless you lower the seat. It's pretty easy. Just climb up there and bring it down a couple of links."

The kid stared up at the hook where the

chains holding the seat connected to the frame of the swing set. "I'd need a ladder to do that." He turned to Joel and visually measured him. "You could reach it."

Joel considered the cross bar of the frame. "I can try it."

Buddy hopped off the swing seat and braced his hands on his jean-clad hips. "Try it." He made a hopeful face. "Please."

Thirty or so seconds later the seat was lowered by three links of chain on either side. "Try that out."

He settled in the seat, no hopping in required this time, and shuffled his cowboy boots over the grass. He grinned at Joel as he launched into a wide swing.

The new squeals were thanks enough.

When Buddy had slowed to a relaxed back and forth motion, Joel broached a few questions. Better to ask the stickier ones without his mom around. "The grandmother lady was nice, huh? Did she give you a present?"

"Yep she was nice. And funny, too. She promised to bring me a present next time."

"Did she tell you her name?"

"Nope." He kicked at the grass. "She said it was okay to call her grandma."

Uneasiness settled heavy in Joel's gut. "Did she talk to your uncle Tater?"

"Nope. Just me. She was busy washing dishes."

Took some nerve to waltz in through the back door of an establishment and just pretend to work there.

"Your mom ever talk to you about not talking to strangers?"

"She wasn't a stranger. She was nice."

That was what he figured. "Maybe next time you see her you can introduce her to your mom or to me first."

"She's shy. She doesn't like to talk to people she doesn't know. Just me and Mr. Bear."

Joel had seen the crime-scene photos from when the Barkers were arrested. The middle daughter Lisa—Laney—had had a teddy bear exactly like the one Buddy lugged around.

He doubted that was coincidence. Laney had most likely been drawn to the bear when she saw it. The mind worked that way sometimes. Even if a memory didn't surface, sensations could be triggered by one or more of the senses.

"Is she coming to see you again?" he asked Buddy.

"Hope so. I want to give her that picture."

Something else he'd have to pass along to Lucas when he arrived in Beaumont.

"I'm ready for juice!" He hopped out of the swing and ran for the back door.

Joel followed. He smiled as the boy shouted for his mom. Reminded him of when his mother was still well enough to be a mom. Many, many years before she died a withered and drawn ghost of the person she had once been. He and his brothers were young. Stair steps, folks called them. Church every Sunday, grace at dinner every night.

In the kitchen, Tatum looked as if he'd lost his best friend. Laney was pouring juice for Buddy, who sat on a stool at the island, boots dangling back and forth. She placed a couple cheese sticks on a napkin, glanced at Joel then Tatum and jerked her head toward the living room.

Joel locked the back door—just in case—before following the two. Maybe the cook had some additional details Laney wanted Joel to know.

If it helped track down Clare Barker, he would be grateful for the info.

Once in the living room, Laney told Tatum, "Tell him what she told you." She nodded toward Joel.

Tatum "Tater" Motley heaved a woeful breath. "She said Laney hired her to come in and help weekends. Wash a few dishes and then go." Tatum glanced at Laney. "Wouldn't be the first time somebody new showed up that I didn't know was coming."

Evidently she had dressed the guy down pretty good.

"From now on whenever I hire anyone new," Laney promised, "I'll make the introductions."

Tatum nodded. "And I'll keep the door locked."

"Sounds like a good plan," Joel noted. He sympathized with the older man. The High Noon hadn't exactly exercised any real security measures. Now probably wasn't a good time to point that out to the boss.

"I'm sorry as I can be that this happened, Laney. You know I love Buddy." The older man shrugged. "But she looked like a nice lady. Harmless."

Might as well take the first step in adopting the deeper cover. Joel fished his cell phone from his front pocket. He pulled up the photo of Clare Barker taken just before her release. He passed it to Tatum.

"Is this the woman who talked to you and Buddy last night?" He hadn't wanted to confuse the kid by showing it to him. A kid that age would think any picture Joel carried around in his pocket had to be of a friend.

Tatum nodded. "Her hair was shorter. But that's her."

Shooting a glare at Joel, Laney reached for the phone. "Let me see that."

Her shoulders seemed to sag as she studied the photo. She might not notice the resemblance at first, but when she'd had time to absorb the details and to think about it, the questions would begin.

Laney thrust the phone at Joel. "Thank you for coming over to discuss this, Tater. I apologize if I overreacted a bit. The whole idea terrifies me."

"Yes, ma'am, I understand. Like I said, I never left Buddy alone with her for a second. But you have my word it won't happen again."

"I know." Laney gave him a hug. "I'll see you tonight."

When the old guy had gone, Joel braced for her interrogation.

She closed the door and turned to him. On him, actually.

Before she could make her first demand, Buddy sauntered into the room and collapsed in the corner with his mound of Legos.

"Coffee?" she asked, her frustration seething under the surface of her cordial tone.

"Sounds good."

He hung his hat on the coatrack near the

front door, made a point to lock it, then wandered into the kitchen. The sound of coffee beans grinding once again delayed the launch of her questioning.

"Why do you have a picture of that woman in your phone?"

He braced his hands on the old butcher counter to prevent crossing his arms over his chest. Any defensive or withdrawn body language would make her all the more suspicious. "The woman's name is Clare Barker. She was released from prison recently and apparently has decided that her best career opportunities can be found working with lowlifes who steal kids and young women for trade. Drugs, money, guns. It's a nasty business."

"So you're not a laid-off security guy, you're a cop." She crossed her arms over her chest, her shoulders back. This was going to be an uphill battle.

"I'm not a cop. I work for a private-investigations agency and I, as well as others, have been hired to keep an eye on potential victims."

Her eyes widened with fear. "Potential victims?"

God, he hated this part. "When it comes to young kids, they're usually looking for certain ages, eye and hair color. Boy versus girl or vice versa."

"I'm absolutely certain that Buddy is not the only five-year-old boy in Beaumont with brown hair and eyes. What made you decide he was in danger?"

Her expression was openly wary now. The cover he'd intended to use was not going to work. That was way too clear to ignore. And the truth was, he didn't want to lie to her.

"All right." He drew in a breath. He was taking a risk here. "I'm not here because of Buddy or any human-trafficking ring." He steeled himself for the disbelief, the anger and then the pain. "He's your son so that makes him my responsibility, too."

"What the hell are you talking about?"

The fight-or-flight response flashed across her face. Keeping her calm was essential. He had to tread carefully here.

"We need to sit down and talk about this." Buddy was in his own little world in the living room but his mother's raised voice would draw him into the room in a heartbeat.

"So talk." There came the anger.

He hadn't given her anything yet to prompt the shock but that was coming. "There are some things I need to get from my Jeep, then we can sit down and go over the facts you don't know about your past."

She stormed out of the kitchen. Joel followed her into the living room where she snatched up the cordless handset.

"I'm calling the sheriff."

Buddy looked up.

Joel glanced from him to Laney. "Bring the phone with you. We'll sit on the porch. Hear me out, and then you can call the police if you feel the need."

Several seconds passed before she reacted, most of which she spent eyeing him with something akin to contempt.

"Five minutes," she warned. "Then I'm calling the sheriff and getting some real answers."

He couldn't blame the lady. He'd shown up in her life just days ago and suddenly he was here, in her home, with secrets to reveal. She had every right to be suspicious and angry.

But she had no idea that what he was about to tell her would change her life forever. However complicated her finances and the situation with Kingston were, that was nothing compared to what she was about to learn.

And he couldn't stop it.

"We'll be right outside on the porch if you need anything, Buddy," she said to her son.

He nodded. "I know. Grown-up talk."

Joel smiled. Damn, that kid was smart.

JOEL STRODE OUT to his Jeep. Laney wilted down onto the top step of the porch, the phone clutched in her hand. Part of her wanted to make that call right now. This man—this stranger—had been too good to be true and she had known it.

"Damn you, Laney," she muttered.

She thought she'd learned her lesson when it came to trusting the wrong guys and here she was about to be scammed for God only knew what reason.

Her fingers tightened around the handset. But he'd taken care of Terry... He'd watched her house all night. And then he'd gotten rid of that damned bank appraiser. Was all of that nothing more than an act?

Instinct warned that if Hayden was up to no good it was motivated by the Kingstons. To her knowledge she had no other enemies. Her banker was likely getting his palm greased with Kingston money, too.

Every single problem she had could be traced back to that crazy short-lived relationship with Terry. What an idiot she had been!

No. No. That doomed relationship had given her Buddy. She hadn't been a total idiot. Or maybe God had known she needed an angel to help her rise above the troubles in her life.

Hayden joined her on the porch, settling next

to her. After the way she'd watched him play with Buddy she'd started to feel more comfortable with letting her guard down a little more.

He carried a case, like a portfolio. Black leather. Much larger than the one the appraiser had carried. His body language told her that whatever he had to say he wasn't looking forward to doing so. What could this stranger possibly know about her past?

Wait. He'd said he worked for a private-investigations agency.

"Before you start," she said, cutting him off when he would have spoken, "I'd like to see some kind of credentials."

He dug out his wallet and showed her his Texas driver's license which identified him as Joel Grant Hayden of Houston, Texas. Then he pulled out another picture ID which showed he was an investigator for the Colby Agency.

"I can give you the number if you feel inclined to call."

She hadn't checked his references. Too much had happened. "What's in the case?"

He opened the leather case and removed a photo album. "Did your parents tell you or leave a will informing you that you had been adopted?"

An old but familiar terror trickled into her veins. "No. Of course not. Why would they?"

She banished those old feelings that hadn't haunted her in years.

"When you were almost four you and your two sisters were taken—"

"Sisters?" She stood, moved down the two steps and glared at him. She couldn't sit and listen to this. "I don't have any sisters."

"You do. Two. One younger, one older. Both right here in Texas."

"You must have me mixed up with someone else." She shook her head but there was a distinct storm of uncertainty brewing in her head. "My parents had baby pictures of me from birth." She hugged herself, felt suddenly cold despite the warm midday sun.

"The attorney who handled the private adoptions was in Austin. When the woman came to him with the three girls to be adopted, she provided baby photos for all three of you."

"That doesn't make any sense. Why would anyone do that?" She shook her head. This was nonsense. Crazy. "And why split us up?"

"There are a lot of questions I can't answer." He tapped the album in his lap. "This will help but there are some things you may never know."

"What about the woman who—" she shook her head "—had the photos and supposedly did all this?"

"She was murdered six days ago."

Fear sparked anew. "What? Murdered?" She held up her hands, the phone still clutched in one. "This is like something from a bad movie."

"Why don't I start from the beginning?"

"Start wherever you like but I think there's been a mistake." Denial and fear and other emotions she couldn't even label twisted wildly inside her.

"Twenty-six years ago you were born Lisa Barker. Parents Clare and Rafe Barker of Granger, Texas."

She stood still as stone, his words echoing in her soul. This was impossible and yet some part of her couldn't refute the words. Sounds and sensations continued to echo.

"Your father was a veterinarian. Your mother his assistant. The five of you lived in an old sprawling farmhouse. The barn had been remodeled into the office and clinic for your father."

Images too vague and dark tumbled one over the other through her head. She blinked them back. This whole thing was like mass hysteria or something. She was only feeling this way because he sounded so convincing. He was wrong. He had to be wrong.

"When you were almost four, your parents

were about to be arrested. Your father claims he wanted to protect the three of you so he whisked you away in the middle of the night and left the three of you in the hands of a family friend with instructions to see that you were taken care of. He alleges that he wanted you to have happy lives free of the Barker name and legacy."

"What legacy?" Claims? Alleges? Why was he talking like that? "You talk as if this man is still alive."

"They both are. Rafe is in Polunsky Prison awaiting execution. His wife, Clare, was on death row in another prison but her conviction was recently overturned so she's free."

Goose bumps started to crawl along her skin. "What were they convicted of?"

"Multiple homicides. Rafe and Clare are the 'Princess Killers.'"

Laney felt the color drain from her face. In the middle of the night once when she couldn't sleep she had watched some true-crime special about criminals of Texas. That couple had been the stars of the show. "They killed all those little girls?"

Hayden nodded.

Wait! Laney remembered something else from the show. "They killed their own daughters, too." Ha! She had known there had to be a mistake. "How could I be one of their daughters when I'm obviously alive?"

"As I said, Rafe claims he had the three of you taken to safety and he made it look as if you were murdered. He insists Clare was the murderer and that he was protecting the three of you."

He'd said that. Yes. But he had to be wrong. "If that's true, why is Clare free and he still awaiting execution?"

"He never said a word in his own defense during trial. His goal was to keep his daughters safe even if it meant execution. Clare insisted the entire time she was innocent. She finally won an appeal."

"Okay." Laney started to pace. "Why is your agency involved in this? Why track me down now after all these years—if you can even prove what you say?"

"Rafe claims his wife wanted the three of you dead. He broke his silence after more than twenty years to contact our agency after Clare was released. He begged us to find the three of you and protect you from her."

"Sounds like he just wants a ticket off death row," she argued. No way this could be about her. She had no sisters. Maybe she was adopted. She'd had freaky dreams when she was kid. Sometimes even now. But this was way off the charts unbelievable.

"He says he has no interest in clearing his name. He only wants his daughters protected."

"Show me your proof." She sat down next to him and reached for the photo album.

The first page opened to a newborn photo and a birth certificate for Lisa Barker. She pointed to it. "That doesn't prove a thing."

He said nothing, just let her keep looking.

As she turned the pages, Laney felt the bottom drop from her stomach. The pictures were all of her. Duplicates of what her parents had had in their family albums. Maybe not duplicates but photos taken from the same time frame.

The photos of her as a toddler with a man and a woman took her breath. She pointed to the couple. "That's them...the Barkers."

She remembered vividly the photos of the couple on the television show. It had been one of those investigative shows. The woman—Clare—had even granted an interview. But not the man. The woman...

Laney turned to Hayden. "That was her." The words were scarcely a whisper. "She came into the High Noon and talked to my son."

"I'm afraid so."

Her hands shaking, Laney flipped through

the pages that showed snapshots in time of her life up until now—the good, the bad and the ugly. How was it that someone had gotten close enough to take these pictures and her not have known it?

When she reached the final page, packed with photos from her renovations on the house and the saloon, she quickly closed it and handed it back to him as if it were poison.

And it was.

She stared forward, at nothing at all. He was telling the truth. Dear God. All she had thought she knew… The entire foundation of her life was a deception.

"What does she want?" The voice that came out of her sounded nothing like hers.

"According to her estranged husband, Clare wants to find each of you and do what was supposed to have been done twenty-two years ago."

Ice closed around her heart. She turned to him, stared straight into his eyes. "She wants us dead."

"We can't confirm that's her goal, and until we do it's imperative that you're protected twenty-four/seven."

"And that's why you're here. To provide protection."

His face grim, he nodded.

"For how long?" There was no way to even guess how long it would be before this woman was stopped.

Was she really buying into this? She blinked back the images she had seen in the album. How could she not?

"As long as it takes."

Chapter Seven

Laney went back inside her house.

Joel stood. He hadn't wanted to tell her right away. Too much risk that she would go to the authorities or make some other move that would get the media's attention.

The less Clare Barker knew about her daughters, the better. Keeping the situation contained until a resolution was reached was absolutely essential. Warden Prentice at Polunsky Prison and the Texas State D.A.'s office wanted this investigation off the record until the puzzle was solved.

He climbed the steps wishing there was something he could say to make this easier but there was not.

Laney would have to come to terms with this nightmare in her own time. At the moment he felt confident that her priority was protecting her son. If Clare was desperate to get at Laney, she might not think twice about using her son.

If the woman was innocent, which seemed highly doubtful after her escape from surveillance and the steps she had taken since, last night was the first time she'd seen her grandson. She may not have known until she tracked Laney down that she had a grandchild.

But there were two looming questions. Why had she evaded Lucas's surveillance? And how had she found Laney? There was no positive proof as of yet that she had tracked down Sadie, her youngest. But there was no doubt this time.

Clare Barker was here and she was growing bolder.

Since Laney left the door ajar, Joel figured it was safe to go inside without knocking. Laney sat on the sofa. Buddy was still occupied with his building project.

Joel placed the photo album on the steamer-trunk-turned-coffee-table and took a seat in a chair across from her. He doubted she wanted him too close, and from the blank expression on her face, talking wasn't on her mind, either.

Buddy wandered over to the sofa. "I'm ready for lunch," he announced. "Breakfast was a long time ago."

"Come on, big guy." Joel stood and rubbed the kid's head. "Since your mom made breakfast, why don't we whip up lunch?"

Buddy looked from his mom to Joel. "Why do we have to whip it? Whippings are bad."

Joel laughed. "You got me on that one, Buddy."

Laney didn't say a word as they left the room. Damn, this had to be hard.

Buddy went straight to the fridge. He opened the door, then dragged one of the chairs over so he could stand on it and survey the offerings.

"No baloney. No cheese. No ham."

He continued naming off the unacceptable options lining the shelves. Joel had a feeling this was going to turn into an ordeal.

The kid turned to Joel. "Can you make sk'hetti?" He leaned closer and whispered, "Not the stuff in the cans."

"Possibly." Unless there was bottled sauce on hand, that might be a no-go.

Joel checked the cabinets. To his relief he discovered a jar of warm-and-serve sauce. And pasta. They were in business.

Buddy had already climbed on the island and retrieved the necessary pot and pan.

Joel watched as he carefully climbed back onto the chair and down to the floor. Instead of dragging the chair back to the table, he scooted it over to the pantry.

"We gotta have something green. Lunch and dinner has to have green."

By green Joel presumed he meant a vegetable. "Got any green beans in there?"

Buddy went from door to door perusing the supplies. "No green beans but we got spargut." He made a face. "Takes like yuck but it's green."

Asparagus. The kid was right. It did taste like yuck from a can. Roasted or grilled, fresh was best.

Joel had the water on to boil and the sauce and asparagus in pans when Laney appeared. She looked emotionally drained and her arms were still wrapped around her waist. Drained and shaken. The entire structure of her life had just been jerked from beneath her feet.

"Buddy, why don't you go finish your project and start figuring out what you'll take to the High Noon this evening?"

Buddy frowned. "But I'm cooking." He had dragged his chair over next to Joel and stood in the seat to watch his every move.

"I think Mr. Hayden has it under control."

Buddy huffed a big breath. "More grown-up talk."

He hopped down and dragged his chair back to the table. "I want to help drain the noodles, please."

"I'll let you know when they're ready," Joel promised.

Satisfied, Buddy shuffled off to do as he was told.

"What are the police doing about this?" she asked without preamble.

He leaned against the counter near the stove so he could see when the water started to boil. "They aren't involved yet."

"Why not?"

Time for the anger. "We have no evidence. All we have is the allegations of a man on death row who may be jealous that his wife got off and he didn't."

"But she came into my saloon and talked to my son," Laney argued. "That's trespassing or something."

"And she's gone. We can't prove it was her. It was a woman who looked like her is all we can claim. We have no idea where she is. We can't connect her to having broken the law. She can do as she pleases until she crosses that line."

"The bottom line," Laney said as she squared her shoulders, "is that you have no idea what her intent is."

"We can only speculate based on her husband's allegations and her actions since being released. But we're not willing to take the risk that she is an innocent woman who only wants to be reunited with her children. If the only thing she wanted to do was talk to you, she had the opportunity. But she didn't."

She rubbed at her forehead. "So no one can stop her?"

"Until she breaks the law, all we can do is watch her."

"Why wasn't someone watching her last night?"

"A few nights ago she gave the man watching her the slip and until now we couldn't be sure where she was. But, trust me, every effort is being made to get her back on the radar."

Laney moved closer to him, leaned against the counter on the opposite side of the stove. "If it's true that she killed those girls, she could be capable of anything."

"That's why we can't take any chances."

"So you're asking me to allow you to stay with us every minute until this situation is resolved?"

"Call the Colby Agency and those references I gave you. I'm here to help, Laney. I know it's difficult to trust someone you've known only for a few days. I wish I could make you see that there simply is no other way to do this."

"Give me those numbers again."

"I'll do you one better." He handed her his cell phone. "Call anyone in my contact list.

Ask anything you want to ask. Then make your decision."

She stared at him for a good long while, then she accepted his phone and walked away. He heard the front door close as he dumped the pasta into the boiling water and then added a dash of olive oil. He'd learned that trick from his older brother. Kept the noodles from sticking together.

He set the flame under the sauce and the asparagus. He'd noticed lemonade in the fridge. It wasn't wine but then his assignment had just elevated to a new hazard level. Extra precaution was needed.

Clare Barker was here.

"Hey, Buddy! You want to give me a hand in here?" It wasn't time to drain the pasta but there were a few things they could get ready.

The kid set the table while Joel monitored the stove.

Once the pasta was drained and the meal was transferred to serving dishes, they were ready.

Laney was still outside.

Joel helped Buddy get his plate ready and ensured he was settled at the table before going in search of her.

He crossed the porch and sat down on the swing next to her.

She handed him his phone. "I should not only trust you, I should marry you."

He frowned. "I'm afraid to ask who gave you that advice."

"One of your brothers. The oldest I think."

"Yeah, he bugs me about being single all the time. Especially now that they're all married except me."

"Why aren't you married?" She pushed against the floor with the toe of her boot and set the swing in motion.

"Never ran into a lady who made me want to divert from the status quo. I like my life."

"You mean you're afraid of change."

He laughed. "I'm not afraid of change."

"That's what they all say." She stopped the swing and got to her feet. At the steps she leaned against the porch post and stared out over her yard.

He studied her a moment. "Does this mean you will accept my offer of protection?"

"I don't really have a choice, do I?"

"I wish I could give you a different answer but I can't. The situation is escalating and I need to ensure you and Buddy stay safe."

She stared at her hands a moment. "From the moment Buddy was born the only thing I wanted was to make sure he was safe and happy. And now everything's going to hell because of my mistakes."

"This isn't your mistake, Laney." He came to her, took one of her hands in his and gave it a squeeze to get her to look at him. "You can't help who your parents are or what they do."

She nodded, didn't try to tug her hand from his. "But I sure screwed everything else up. I'm probably going to lose our home and my business." She glanced out at the old truck in the driveway. "I never thought I'd have to resort to making Old Blue home again."

"Never surrender, Laney. The battle isn't over until you win or you give up."

"Easy for you to say."

He hitched his head toward the door. "Come on. Sk'hetti and spargut will do you good."

She laughed but the emotion shining in her eyes told him she felt more like crying than laughing.

They made it just inside the door when the house phone rang.

With a weary sigh, Laney answered.

Joel checked on Buddy, who had spaghetti sauce all over his face. He smiled. "I guess we make a pretty good team."

The kid nodded. "'cept for the spargut."

Laney appeared at the kitchen door. "That

was the Beaumont police. Vandals hit the High Noon last night. The officer said it's pretty bad."

Damn. Couldn't the lady get a break?

3:05 p.m.

A COUPLE OF WINDOWS were broken. Ugly words were scrawled in white paint across the antique front door that opened into the lobby-style entry. Big splats of paint stained the wood walkway that ran across the front of the saloon.

That was the good part.

Inside, several chairs were broken—eight if she counted right. Two tables were damaged.

Dozens of liquor bottles were shattered, their contents soaking into the old hardwood floor.

The kitchen and office had been spared. The latter was the strangest part of all. Why didn't they tear the office apart looking for money?

Fury tightened Laney's jaw. Because it wasn't about money. This was Terry's kind of tactic. She doubted he would have the guts to do it himself, but one of his scumbag friends would be only too happy to wreak such damage.

Hayden had already started sweeping up the broken glass from the liquor bottles. Buddy was seated at one of the untouched tables playing an electronic learning game.

Laney needed paint remover to scrub the slurs from the door. The rest of the cleanup would be more about manual labor.

She'd have to make do with fewer tables and chairs until she had the cash to buy some replacements. But the liquor supply would have to be taken care of immediately.

Outside, Terry's car still sat in the lot. That was the only part that mystified her. If he'd put someone up to this, why leave his car? Maybe to make it look as if he hadn't been back. But then why hadn't the vandals touched his fancy car?

The police had made the report, but doubted their efforts would be anything but futile considering the crowd in and out of here every night. Thousands of fingerprints and loads of trace evidence but nothing that would likely help find the lowlife who had done this. Her money was on Terry, but Hayden had a different theory.

Laney's insurance would cover the damages but the darned deductible was so high that she would be better off not even filing a claim.

"I need to get some paint remover." She opened at six. There was no time to stand around here pretending the cleanup would get done on its own. Even if the doors had to be sanded and restained, they were opened and pushed against the walls during operating hours, except in the winter. The Old West style swinging doors that separated the lobby from the saloon hadn't been touched. Thank God.

"I already called the nearest hardware store. They're delivering the paint remover and some shop towels," Hayden told her. "I also called the supply store and someone is pulling together a liquor supply run based on what you typically order."

He called and asked for a delivery? No, two deliveries. Laney had no idea something as simple as paint remover was a deliverable item. Maybe he'd promised a big tip which would greatly impact her pocketbook.

But she wasn't about to complain. She needed his help.

"Thanks."

Tater would be here within the hour to help.

Grabbing a bucket, gloves and cleaning clothes, she started with the liquor shelves and counter. Whoever had done this hadn't exactly been methodical which was to her benefit. Just random damage as if the person or persons who'd done it had been angry.

Had to be Terry. Jerk.

She checked for her Louisville Slugger behind the bar. A friend had given the bat to her when she first opened the saloon. *If you ever have any trouble, this'll do the trick.* Laney smiled. So far she'd never had to use it. Buddy had asked her a dozen times why he couldn't play with it.

Hayden was right. She needed to introduce her son to sports.

Her son. At least Buddy knew who his parents were.

She had been adopted.

The emotional wallop came out of nowhere and made her quake inside. Why hadn't her parents told her? Maybe they would have if they hadn't died so suddenly.

She tugged the gloves onto her hands, stared at them a moment. How could she be the biological result of two killers? Was that why she'd gotten into so much trouble in her teen years? Was she bad deep down inside?

Laney shook off the horrible thoughts and focused on the work. Her parents had died when she was ten. These other people—Rafe and Clare—were not her parents. Just the reproductive donors.

Something else to protect her son from.

The sound of tires spinning in the gravel outside drew her attention to the door just in time to see Terry swagger in. Judging by his walk he was already well on his way to intoxication at this early hour.

"I need my keys," he shouted. "Hey, Buddy boy."

Buddy glanced up, then lowered his face closer to the screen of his game.

Laney stripped off her gloves and snagged his keys from under the bar. Joel set his broom aside but Laney stopped him with a look. "I've got this.

"You see this mess?" she demanded.

Terry glared at her as if she were a lesser life-form.

"Did you do this, Terry?"

He looked around as if for the first time. "You know when I left last night." Terry shot her another of those condescending looks. "I haven't been back until now. Now give me my keys."

Later, Laney would look back on this moment and still the reason she lost it so completely would elude her.

She tossed the keys to him. He missed the catch, of course. She waited until he'd swaggered out and then she did what she had wanted to do for years.

Louisville Slugger in hand, she strode out the door with Hayden calling her name.

With Terry fumbling with his keys, she walked right up and swung. The impact left a fair-size dent in the hood of his prized car. She moved on to the windshield.

"What the hell are you doing?" he screamed.

Laney made her way around the car, bashing windows, denting metal.

Terry rushed around to her and started wrestling for control of the bat. The desire to use it on his head was nearly more than she could resist.

Suddenly Hayden was there. She had a feeling he could have stepped in earlier but decided not to spoil her fun.

Hayden gained control of the bat and held it aside. With the other hand he manacled Terry by the collar. "It would be in your best interest not to come here again."

"You touch me and my father will make sure you regret it."

Hayden shoved him aside. "Tell him not to waste the effort. I already regret it. Now go and do not come back without making arrangements with Laney."

"Finally got you another guy," Terry accused. "I see how it is." He sent an accusing look at Laney. "I don't care what you do but you will not keep my son from me."

Laney got right in his face. "I don't have to. You're doing a stellar job yourself. No judge with half a brain is going to entertain your petition of custody with your record."

"You mean like he's going to entertain the idea of a kid hanging around a bar all night every night?"

Before Laney could do something even more stupid, Hayden pressed the bat to Terry's chest. "I'm certain you want to keep breathing. Now go."

"This is nothing compared to what you've got coming," Terry threatened. "Watch your back, Laney!"

He climbed into his car and revved the engine. Despite the cracked glass and dents, he spun out of the lot.

Good riddance.

Hayden turned on her, fury flashing in those bronze eyes. If he'd been gripping the bat any tighter it might have splintered. "This isn't a .32," Hayden warned. "When you attack a guy's vehicle, you attack him. No more of this, Laney. It could have gone way wrong."

Now she was mad all over again. He had no right to tell her how to conduct her personal life. They weren't in a relationship. As much as she appreciated him being here considering what he'd revealed to her this morning, she didn't need him deciding what was best for her.

"I need you because of this other crap, but

I don't need you to tell me how to protect my kid or my property."

With the truth in his words stinging her cheeks despite her proclamation, she wheeled around and stalked back into the saloon. She had plenty to do that didn't involve discussing the subject of her ex or her son with him or anyone else. She yanked the gloves back on and set to the work of cleaning up the mess behind the bar.

Hayden walked into the saloon a few minutes later, wagging the paint remover and plenty of cleaning rags. Like her, he had gotten worked up over this whole mess. He'd probably been out there cooling off.

"I can work on the paint if you can finish up here."

That was exactly her point. The man thought he was the boss and they'd hardly done more than hold hands. She could only imagine how territorial he would be if they'd so much as kissed. Why was it guys always thought they knew best?

"Whatever." This whole day had just been too much.

The plunk of items on the counter made her jump but she didn't turn around. When he invaded her space behind the counter she had no choice but to meet his fierce gaze.

"You've done a fine job raising your son," he said, the words tight with restrained tension. "I just don't want you getting hurt any more than you already have by that deadbeat guy."

His expression relaxed just a little. He looked away before she could analyze the change further.

"I appreciate your concern." She surrendered. "It made me angry that you were right. I lost control and that was a mistake. I just didn't want to admit it."

He touched her arm. It was nothing really. Just a simple slide of his fingers down the length of her upper arm from shoulder to elbow, but the heat that blazed inside her was not simple at all. She was attracted to this man. Had been since he walked through those swinging doors that first night.

She couldn't go there. The move would have been dumb enough before but it was downright foolish now. His revelation this morning had stolen something from her. The certainty of who she was and where she'd come from. She couldn't handle anything else.

"You've had a lot dumped on you when you were already carrying more than your share. I wish I hadn't been the one to do the dumping. But this is not going away until we learn the truth. I need you to use caution in all you do."

She nodded. "I understand. It'll take some time for me to get my head on straight." She wished he wasn't so nice. Maybe then she wouldn't feel like a complete idiot for going stupid in the parking lot.

"We'll get this place back in shape and you do what you do." He smiled and her knees went a little weak. "I'll have your back and I'll help Tatum keep an eye on Buddy."

Laney closed her eyes and fought the urge to cry. That was the part that terrified her the most. She needed to know her baby was safe. As torn up as she was at learning her life was one big fabrication, his safety was all that really mattered.

Hayden's fingers tightened around her arm. "Trust me, Laney. That's all I'm asking."

He had no idea what a monumental request that was for her. Trusting him to do his job was easy. Actions spoke louder than words and she had seen in him action. But that personal trust she sensed he wanted as well was a whole different arena, one where she'd made the wrong decision too many times already.

"I'll give it my best shot."

Chapter Eight

5:00 p.m.

The house was pretty.

It reminded Clare of the one where she had raised her children…until *that day*.

The sickening ingredients of fear and hatred stirred into the pot of misery simmering inside her. *He* had taken all of that from her.

She could not change the past but the future was hers. Clare was free and in twenty-four days *he* would be dead. Her soul would rejoice.

If there was any justice in the universe he would burn in hell for all eternity. It would almost be worth joining him there just to watch him fry. She wished she could watch him gasp for his last desperate breath, but that was impossible.

Her mission had only just started. She had those same twenty-four days to see her goal accomplished. Rage kindled deep in her belly when she considered that *he* had so many on his side. The Colby Agency in particular. They were strong and smart. But they would not stop Clare.

She had almost been stuck in that rat hole of an apartment in Copperas Cove. But a blessing in the form of rescue had come at just the right moment.

Clare turned to Tony. What a good man he had become. No thanks to her.

"You're not safe here." He studied the house and its nice plot of property. "They could come back."

Clare smiled. "I think they'll be too busy to come back. You did a good job." Maybe too good but she wouldn't scold him for showing ambition.

Tony ducked his head. "I promised I would. I was careful this time."

"Let's hide the car and have a look inside."

He scowled. "That might be dangerous."

"Hmm. I don't think so. There's no security system. The house is old. Getting in should be very easy." She gifted her firstborn with a reassuring smile. "And I have you. What could go wrong?"

Reluctantly he obeyed. Farther up the road was a turnoff that led to nowhere. Just one of those places added for turning around or for hunters perhaps since it only led a few yards into the woods. These old country roads were full of little niches like that.

From there she and Tony marched through the field. The sun felt good on Clare's face. She had lived in that ugly gray cell for so many years. Her youth had vanished in the darkness of that awful place. Nearly half her life. But that was behind her now. She was free. And nothing was going to stop her from making them pay.

One already had.

Clare wrapped her arm around Tony's. He had made sure no one could harm her. He was a far better son than she deserved. If he only knew what she had suffered before his birth he would understand. But she dared not tell him for fear that the ugly truth would only add to his own suffering.

They had both suffered far too much.

It was time for the rest to suffer.

She had ensured Gus Gilmore could no longer keep his secret. Sadie was not his daughter. He had pretended all these years that she belonged to him. He'd given her a new name— Sadie, of all things—and kept the truth from her all those years. In a moment of heated emotions she had called him and warned that she was coming for her baby girl, but that had been wrong of her. Still, now Clare's baby girl knew the truth. And one day soon they would be together.

She squeezed Tony's arm. They would all be together.

"We'll try the back door."

"Whatever you think."

Tony was smart, too. He'd gone to school to be a nurse. He'd used that skill to get to that devil waiting on death row for his time to come. Tony had promised to take care of Clare now that she was free and they were reunited. With him and her three girls, the rest of her days would be filled with happiness.

A mother should be happy. Memories of locked doors and darkness...of her girls crying out for her tore at her heart. Never again... Never again.

With just a minute of manipulating Tony had the back door open. Clare entered the kitchen of her middle daughter and felt right at home. Her kitchen smelled of frequent use. Spices and the aroma of something recently baked. A plate of leftover biscuits sat on the counter.

Clare tasted one. "Mmm." Made from scratch. "Have a biscuit, Tony. Your sister made them."

He shook his head, too bashful to be so bold as Clare. She understood. He had spent his life cowering in fear. That was her fault. She intended to make that up to him.

Clare wandered to the fridge and admired her grandson's artwork. "He's like you, Tony." She turned to him. "Gifted."

One of those rare smiles lifted his lips. "He's a fine-looking boy."

"He is."

Clare made her way through each room. She studied the framed photographs and touched the things that held a place in her daughter's and grandson's lives. A good, comfortable home.

Tony hovered near the front windows, nervous about being caught. Lisa and this man from the Colby Agency were too busy to worry about anything else just now.

In Buddy's room, Clare sat down at his little desk and drew him a picture with the crayons and craft paper. When she was finished, she put everything back exactly as it had been. Then she placed the picture on her grandson's pillow.

"Just for you," she said softly. There were so many things they would soon be able to do together.

In Laney's room she found a photo album with oodles of pictures of her and Buddy. Clare took one and slipped it into her pocket. She hated to steal from her own daughter but she wanted desperately to have something to remember her by. She had one of Sarah already.

Tony had handled the situation there a bit poorly. He had left that ugly message to frighten the girl. Clare had chastised him for doing such a thing. He'd sworn that he hadn't set fire to her house but Clare worried that he might have accidently caused the fire and then feared telling her.

Since no one was harmed, she decided not to torture him about it. He had suffered enough.

With a deep sigh of contentment, Clare joined her son in the living room and took his hand.

"Let's be on our way. We have much to do."

No one would stop Clare from reuniting with her daughters. Rafe was going to pay anyway…far more than he knew. And that Victoria woman and her agency had better stay out of Clare's way or she would pay, too.

Chapter Nine

5:51 p.m.

Lucas had been in Beaumont less than three hours and already he had canvassed most of the hotels, motels and any other dives advertising rooms for rent.

He'd prioritized his list by the ones with the least visibility.

Victoria was worried. She would have preferred that he stay at the office and that one of the agency's new recruits have taken this task.

But this job belonged to Lucas. It was his responsibility that Clare Barker had jumped off the radar. He had fallen down on the job and now others were at risk. Lyle McCaleb had Sadie Gilmore under close watch; no problem there. But Olivia Westfield was not fully covered at this time. St. James was still watching her from a distance. Joel Hayden had shown Laney the photo album and explained the risks but it was yet to be seen whether Laney would go for around-the-clock, up-close-and-personal protection.

She had no idea how badly she needed that kind of security.

At least one person was dead. Whether Clare Barker, which was highly unlikely since Lucas had been watching her apartment at the time, or Tony Weeden committed the murder—and Lucas suspected it was the latter—dead was dead.

Lucas pulled into the parking lot of the next motel from his Yellow Pages list. Another dive, but those types presented the lowest profile and required the least in the way of identification for anyone looking to stay under the radar.

The air was cooling down, a nice contrast to the unusually warm day. He'd already made his own arrangements to bunk in the office at the High Noon. Clare's appearance at the saloon as well as the vandalism had ensured Laney's co-operation. Hayden said Laney kept a cot in the office for her son. That would work. He wanted as close as possible. Particularly since vandals had hit the saloon at some point this morning.

Both he and Hayden understood that this was most likely the work of Clare Barker's sidekick but convincing the police, or Laney for that matter, without evidence wasn't likely to happen in time to reap any benefit.

Also because of the vandalism at the saloon, the police had offered to make extra drive-bys the next few days but that was the best they could do until they had a lead on a suspect.

Lucas entered the motel office. The manager looked up from the book he was reading. A small fan sat on the counter stirring the stale air.

"I'll need a driver's license and cash up front," the man informed him. "No credit cards."

Lucas moved to the counter, his limp a little more pronounced than usual. He'd spent too much time behind the wheel today. "I'm not looking for a room."

The guy set his book aside. "You a cop?"

"No need to get into the technicalities." Lucas passed him the photos of Clare Barker and Tony Weeden. "Have you seen either of those two? Maybe they rented a room."

The manager nodded. "I saw him all right." He shook his head and handed the photos back to Lucas. "Felt sorry for him because of the missing arm. Even gave him a discount. Sorry sack of—"

"Is he still registered here?" Anticipation sharpened.

"Nah. They cleared out this morning, but they left a hell of a mess for me to deal with."

"Have you cleaned the room already?"

"No use cleaning it. It's gonna need a new paint job."

"Can I see the room?"

The other man's eyebrows reared up. "I figured you was a cop." He grabbed a key, the old-fashioned kind attached to a plastic placard sporting the room number.

Outside, the twelve rooms were divided in half by the office. A row of six fanned out on either side. The motel was a one-story place with little recognizable landscaping and even less visible upkeep. Shabby.

Room ten sat near the end to the left of the office. Lucas followed the manager to the door, his aching leg forgotten.

"Yeah, the cleaning lady came into the office raising cane this morning. I figured it was the usual kind of mess. Drugs, alcohol or some freaky sex-party leftovers." He hesitated before opening the door. "Didn't expect this."

He pushed the door inward and motioned for Lucas to have a look.

Dozens of stick-figure drawings littered the walls. Some were what appeared to be three little girls in a row. Others featured the three girls along with a mother and a larger male stick figure. Some had a sixth stick figure, this one much smaller. Clare, her three grown daughters, Weeden and the grandchild.

Dread settled in Lucas's gut.

"The freak used a felt-tip marker that won't scrub off. It'll take some work to cover that up."

Lucas surveyed each drawing. All were meticulously drawn. Then, as if the artist had decided the work wasn't right, he'd come along and hastily slashed each one with a large X.

Whether it was Clare or Weeden, Lucas couldn't be sure. Whichever it was, they were dealing with one very sick individual. Or maybe they were both over the edge.

Either way, in Lucas's opinion, the desperation of the situation was intensifying. The urgency or hatred one or both of the suspects felt was obvious.

It was only a matter of time before the urgency evolved into sheer desperation…. And then anything could happen.

Chapter Ten

High Noon Saloon, 11:15 p.m.

Joel joined Lucas at the table farthest from the rowdy crowd gathered around the jukebox. Considering it was a Monday night it was hard to believe any one of these folks had to go to work in the morning.

The beer was flowing and the music was loud. Most were either dancing or huddled in throngs talking and laughing. So far nothing but good clean fun. And no sign of Kingston, which Joel appreciated. As much as the guy deserved to have some good sense beat into him, he was still Buddy's father and Joel had no desire to be the one to get the job done.

But he would, if the need arose. The guy wasn't getting another chance to make Laney miserable.

Between the woman getting so close to Buddy and the news Joel delivered today, the dead-last thing she had needed was more hassling from Kingston. The destruction they'd found here was nearly the straw that broke the camel's back. Laney hadn't been herself all night.

She'd rushed to the kitchen, and later the office, so many times to check on Buddy that customer service had suffered. Most had been patient but a few had given her a hard time. Joel had wanted to step in but she'd given him that look that said *back off.* He'd checked on Buddy repeatedly, but no matter how often Joel made his rounds, she had needed to see the boy for herself.

"No word yet on Janet Tolliver's murder?" he asked Lucas. There hadn't been much time to talk. Lucas and Laney had hit it off immediately. He'd even thrown in with her behind the bar as if he'd tended bar his whole life. Joel had no idea the man could draw the draft with such skill.

"Nothing new. Marble angel statue from her own home was the murder weapon, it seems. No prints or other trace evidence discovered so far. The coroner suspects the killer was left-handed. Simon has contacted the great-niece to see if she has any background on the angel." Lucas sipped the same beer he'd been nursing since he took a seat. "Its use as a weapon may or may not be significant."

"Based on what you found in that motel room," Joel suggested, "we may be dealing with a bigger problem than Clare Barker. This Weeden character sounds like he may be a little over the edge."

"There's nothing in his background that suggests a mental disorder. Prentice, the warden at Polunsky Prison, insists Weeden was a stellar employee who never missed a day of work until he disappeared last week. And his background is clean."

"Maybe reading the letter Rafe wrote to Victoria tripped some sort of trigger that sent him over the edge." It happened. A shocking and debilitating illness could lie dormant for the better part of a person's life, only to surface when an intense physical or emotional trauma occurred.

"That's certainly possible," Lucas agreed. "I just hope we can contain it before the onset of more violence."

"The motel manager reported the vandalism?"

"He wasn't going to but I pushed the issue." Lucas checked his cell phone. "I also gave the Copperas Cove police a heads-up on the connection. If the slightest piece of evidence between the motel room and Tolliver's house could be found, we might be about to turn some aspect of this investigation over to the police."

That would take a big load off the Colby Agency. Both Lucas and Victoria were bearing a significant burden with this case. For a retired couple, they worked damned hard. One death during the course of a Colby investigation was one too many.

"Hayden." Mike Kelso, a waiter, paused at their table. "You might want to check what's going on outside. That guy from last night is messing with your Jeep."

"Thanks, Mike. I'm on it. Don't mention this to Laney."

"No prob." The waiter hustled to the next table, the tray loaded with beers balanced in one hand.

"Go ahead," Lucas assured Joel. He pushed to his feet. "I'll check on Buddy and stick close to the bar."

"Appreciate it."

Joel made sure Laney was preoccupied before crossing the room and heading out the door. He didn't want her following.

The parking lot was well lit. A small crowd of onlookers was gathered a safe distance away to watch Terry Kingston wave what appeared to be a tire iron. A blonde female dressed in a super-short skirt, a halter-style top and thigh-high boots was trying to talk him into leaving before trouble started. Evidently her powers of persuasion were proving futile.

Joel cut around behind the arguing couple and approached from the rear.

"Really, baby, let's go," the woman urged. "I can't be caught in no trouble. I still got three months of probation."

Joel came up behind Kingston and snagged the tire iron before he could swing it. "I'd listen to your friend if I were you."

Kingston spun around, stumbled. He stared at his hand and then at Joel's grip on the wrench as if he couldn't understand how the transfer happened.

He looked up at Joel, squared his shoulders and cocked his head. "I don't know who you think you are, but you're messing with the wrong guy, hotshot."

Joel figured Kingston was too drunk then and maybe now to remember anything from the previous night. "Actually, I know exactly who you are and that's my Jeep. So I think you're the one who doesn't understand who you're messing with."

Realization dawned on the man's face. "You may think just because you and Laney have hooked up that you got some say over my son, but you're wrong. I will find a way to get you."

Joel tossed the tire iron aside and grabbed Kingston by the shirt. "We need a word." Holding Kingston far enough away that he couldn't get a swing in, Joel said to his female companion, "Get his keys and drive him to wherever he's staying. If you don't and something happens, I'll make sure the police know you were with him."

Her eyes widened. "I got the keys."

"Good. Where're you parked?"

The woman led the way to another snazzy sports car, this one as nice as the one that was no doubt in the shop after Laney took that Louisville Slugger to it. Kingston tripped and stumbled all the way to the car, mostly in an attempt to connect one of his fists with Joel's face.

Joel slammed the guy against the car, rattled him for a moment. "You listen to me, Kingston. I don't want to have to say this again."

Kingston swore at him. Joel had him pinned to the vehicle so he wasn't moving.

"As long as I'm with Laney," Joel warned, "you'd better stay clear." Before Kingston could interrupt he went on, "I'm not trying to keep you from your son. This—" Joel looked him up and down "—is keeping you from Buddy.

Get smart. Find some help and this time stick with it."

Kingston told him where he could shove his advice.

"This is your mistake to make, pal," Joel cautioned, "but next time I won't be so nice." He released the fool and stepped back. Beating up on a guy too drunk to defend himself would be wrong, even if he deserved it.

Kingston smoothed his hands over his shirt. "I'll be back. You can bank on that." His threat fell short of the mark when he staggered sideways.

"And I'll be here," Joel promised. "Now go before I call your friends in uniform."

Joel waited until Kingston had loaded into the car and his girlfriend had driven away. Despite having won this round, he understood that the fool would be back. When the taillights had faded in the distance, he turned and headed back inside. A round of applause from the crowd of bystanders followed him.

Laney's gaze collided with his and he knew she'd heard about the trouble outside.

LANEY COMPOSED HERSELF and moved on to fill her next order. Hayden looked no worse for the wear. Whatever had happened outside, obviously he'd handled it without violence.

Her hands stilled on the lever as the suds overflowed the glass. Why couldn't Terry get his act together? Her son would need his father at some point and the man lacked the skills to provide that necessary element.

She wiped the foam from her hand and delivered the beer, producing a smile for the customer. Between the bank, Terry and this… other…thing, she was a mess.

With two more beers delivered, she stepped from the bar and hurried to her office to check on Buddy again. He slept like an angel. He had no idea of the storm brewing in their lives.

Careful not to let the latch click too loud, she eased the door shut and joined Mr. Camp. She didn't have the exact chain of command but she got the impression that Camp was Hayden's boss. The man was really something.

When she'd first met him earlier in the evening he'd fooled her. Given his limp and the dark hair peppered thickly with gray, she'd expected the typical old man. Boy, had she been wrong. Lucas was not old by any definition. He was charming and intelligent and a gentleman all the way.

Laney strolled up to him. "We caught up for the moment?"

"We are." He flashed a killer smile, his gray eyes shimmering with kindness. "I think the boss needs a break."

"Oh, I'm sorry. Of course. I can handle this." It was almost midnight. He'd been all over town looking for leads on that woman... Clare Barker. Her mother. Unfamiliar emotions clogged her throat. "I didn't think, Mr. Camp. I'm sure you're exhausted."

The man laughed. "Call me Lucas. And I've got plenty of kick left in me. I meant *you* needed a break."

Laney's hand went to her throat. "Well..." She hadn't sat down all night. Five minutes off her feet would be a blessed relief. "I shouldn't impose."

"Go," he ordered in a tone she doubted few dared to ignore. He nodded toward the far side of the room. "Hayden's holding a seat for you."

"Okay. Five minutes." She started to back away. "If you need me before then—"

Lucas gave her a look and she turned tail and headed through the crowd. Though she had never heard of the Colby Agency, she was definitely impressed. If these two were any indication of the caliber of folks who worked there, they were the best. Her feet slowed as she neared Hayden's table.

He was watching her move toward him and something about the intensity on his face took her breath away. When his gaze made the slow, thorough journey up her body and connected with hers, she stopped. Only a few steps away but she just couldn't make those last three or four strides.

He stood, the movement slow and fluid, and closed the small gap between them. When he was toe-to-toe with her he smiled, stealing her breath all over again.

"You okay?"

She nodded. *I will be as soon as I catch my breath.* "What happened outside?" Truly she didn't want to know. It wouldn't be good. But it was her responsibility to be aware.

One of those sluggish, syrupy country love songs floated from the jukebox and he reached for her. At first she was so startled she couldn't respond. But when he pulled her into his arms her whole body responded.

His arms were strong around her and she felt weak with need. He left the smallest margin of space between them but she closed it. She needed to lean on him. She needed to close her eyes for just a moment and let the rest of the world slip away.

He moved with the rhythm of the music, slow enough they could have been floating on air. His body felt warm and inviting and so powerful. She hadn't been held like this in so long. Maybe she'd never known this sensation of pleasure accompanied by a feeling of safety. She'd been on her own for too long.

She rested her forehead against his jaw. The late-night stubble made her shiver, made her want to reach up with both hands and explore the lean and intriguing contours of his face. She longed to get lost in all these wondrous sensations.... To forget the world.

He stopped moving. Her whole being protested. A couple of seconds were necessary for her to realize why he'd broken the trance.... The music had stopped.

Time and place flooded her senses, washing away the pleasant escape. Humiliation singed her already-flushed face. What had she been thinking? Thankfully no one had stopped to stare. They were just another couple in a packed house.

"I should get back to the bar."

"Take a break in the office with Buddy." Hayden glanced around. "The crowd is thinning. Lucas and I can finish out the night."

Laney started to argue, but he was right. She needed a few minutes away from the demands of the crowd.... Away from how he made her feel.

Tuesday, May 28th, 1:00 a.m.

"LANEY."

Her eyes opened to Hayden leaning over her.

Laney sat up. "Sorry. I guess I dozed off." She'd curled up on the narrow cot with Buddy for just a second.... Or so she'd thought.

"Come on. I'll get Buddy."

"What about cleanup?" Good grief. What had she been thinking? Her staff must be frustrated with her for abandoning them at closing.

"It's all done." He took her hand and pulled her to her feet.

By the time they were loaded in his Jeep, her brain was working again. Everyone had gone for the night. Lucas stood in the doorway watching them go. He would be staying the night.

With her son buckled into his car seat in the backseat and still sound asleep, Laney relaxed and considered that she hadn't allowed herself to collapse like that in ages.

Everything around her felt out of control.

Not that her life had ever been sedate or organized, but usually there was some amount of structure to her chaos. Certainly not now.

"You got the receipts and the cash?" For God's sake, she hadn't even taken care of the books for the night.

"It's all taken care of. You had a particularly good night judging by the previous two or three Mondays' takes."

At least there was some good news. "Thank you."

Funny, she mused. This man had brought a whole new layer of uncertainty and disruption to her life, through no fault of his own, yet he'd also somehow injected a bit of new hope. Not so funny was the idea that she desperately needed him.

Strong, independent, ambitious Laney never needed anyone.

How had that happened in the space of a few short days? However it happened, he was a godsend. She glanced at her hero. Problem was he was only temporary. He was here for his job. So was his boss. She couldn't dare allow herself to get too attached. Laney felt reasonably sure that surviving any more loss and heartache was not in her.

She'd had enough for several lifetimes.

"What's it like…" The words were out of her mouth before she could stop them. She cleared her throat. No point stopping now. "What's it like growing up in a normal family? I mean, past early childhood?"

He glanced at her. "Some days it's a pain but most it's reassuring. You always know you have each other. Even if you have a knock-down drag-out with a sibling, you know if the chips were down, he would be there for you. I can count on my brothers anytime, anyplace."

Since she was ten, Laney hadn't known that kind of support. Since she'd had no siblings—none that she'd known about—she'd missed that special bonding.

"What're they like?"

He glanced at her. "My brothers or your sisters?"

Wow. Sisters. "My sisters."

"Sadie, the youngest, lives in Copperas Cove. She has a small ranch and she rescues horses. Olivia, the oldest, lives in San Antonio. She's a paralegal. She spends a lot of time working for those who can't afford legal aid."

Impressive. "Do we look anything alike?" There had been a couple of photos with her and the others, but only when they were really young.

"Hair color is the same. Sadie's is a little lighter. You and Olivia have the same brown eyes. Sadie's eyes are green like Clare's." He seemed to consider the question a bit. "You're obviously sisters but you're each also unique. You're the tallest. Sadie is kind of petite. Olivia falls somewhere in the middle."

"It's funny. We all rescue something just

like our parents did." The Barkers had rescued cats and dogs. Sadie rescued horses and Olivia those in need of help with legal troubles. Laney rescued things. Old houses. Furniture. All sorts of things. She'd tried to rescue Terry but he'd almost drowned her in the same cesspool he couldn't seem to drag himself out of.

He made the turn into her driveway. "That's because you're all three good people."

For the spawn of cold-blooded killers. But she didn't bother pointing that out.

He shut off the lights and the engine, leaving nothing but the moonlight to illuminate the house. She felt suddenly afraid to go inside for fear of finding some awful message from her recently released-from-death-row mother or her crazy ex.

Not once had she ever thought twice about arriving home at this hour and being afraid.

Hayden was already at her side of the Jeep before she snapped out of the disturbing thoughts. She unbuckled Buddy from his car seat and lifted him into her arms. She walked beside Hayden to the front door. He unlocked it and went inside ahead of her. Once the lights were on, she followed. Those old fears of the dark were back with a vengeance.

He locked the door and checked the kitchen as well as the back door for signs of forced entry before leading her deeper into her own home. A place where she had never felt anything less than safe.

"All clear," he assured her.

Frustrated with herself, she moved ahead of him to Buddy's room. There were only two bedrooms in this old house and the first one as she entered the hall was his. She flipped on the light with her elbow and her little boy's magical realm enveloped her. His things were here. His scent. It was home. Maybe she'd never had siblings or a real family life after the age of ten but she had it now.

She moved to the bed, threw the covers back and snuggled her little boy against his pillow. He burrowed into the soft sheets and never roused. She covered him and kissed his sweet forehead. Yes, this was their home and she would not lose it.

Then and there she decided that she wasn't going to play the victim here. Yes, she had to do as Hayden said until the issues with her biological parents were resolved. But she intended to take charge of this financial crisis. No one was taking hers and Buddy's home.

She moved to the other side of the bed and switched on the night-light. Something crinkled beneath her foot. She looked down and made a face.

Some of Buddy's artwork had fallen on the floor and she'd stepped on it. Dang it!

She picked it up and stared at the drawing. It was different from his usual highly imaginative drawings. Just a row of stick people. The first was obviously a woman. Next to her were two more slightly smaller girl stick figures. Then a little one, a boy since he didn't have the triangle shaped dress. Then another girl stick, the same size as the second and third figures.

How strange.

"What's this?"

Hayden moved to her side and studied the drawing.

"Something Buddy drew…I guess."

Hayden rushed from the room. What the…?

Laney wandered into the hall just as he burst from her bedroom. "What's wrong?"

"Stay right here."

She studied the drawing. Had something about it set him off?

By the time he returned she was more than a little freaked out.

"Someone tampered with the lock on the back door." His face was grim.

"You think someone came in my house?"

He nodded. "Whoever did it was good. He knew what he was doing and left very little evidence of his handiwork. And he locked it when he left."

Laney didn't understand. "Why did this drawing make you feel the need to check the doors again?"

He pulled his cell from his pocket and opened the photo library. "Lucas sent this to me after he found the place where Clare Barker and Tony Weeden stayed last night."

Laney stared at the image in disbelief. Hundreds of stick figures, exactly like the ones in the drawing she'd found in her son's room, marred the walls of the motel room. Only the ones from the motel had been crossed out.

What did this mean?

She stared up at Hayden. "They were here."

He nodded. "They were here."

Chapter Eleven

Beaumont Independent Bank, 10:00 a.m.

The small waiting area outside the bank president's office was nothing more than a hallway, a narrow one at that. On the other side of the glass wall in front of her was the bank's VP guiding a client through a mountain of paperwork. Laney wondered if that client, too, would be sitting here a few years from now wondering what would happen next.

Behind Laney was the president's office. She noted a client in his office when she'd taken her seat. Obviously that appointment was running long. The delay gave her a few minutes more to bolster her courage.

She understood that times were hard, but why make it even more difficult for a working woman to keep her head above water? Whatever happened to teamwork?

Speaking of which, Joel Hayden had happily agreed to take Buddy across the street for ice cream at the Dairy Dip. How had she gotten so lucky to have a man like him show up in her life at this pivotal moment?

No, luck had nothing to do with it. Evidently it was fate. And fate had taken its sweet time pulling this particular rug from under her feet.

How could she be twenty-six years old and not know who she was in the literal sense? Maybe her adopted parents had intended to tell her when she was older. Or maybe they'd never intended to tell her at all.

The idea that she was the daughter of convicted murderers lowered her already-sinking self-esteem down into the vicinity of her boots. The only saving grace that she could see was that she had two sisters. Buddy had aunts.

It was all a little overwhelming. Who was she kidding? It was a lot overwhelming. Not only could she and Buddy possibly be in danger, but once the media got wind of what was going on there would be fallout, too. Buddy started school this fall. Would the other kids make fun of him for being the grandson of Texas's most notorious killers?

Would business at the High Noon dwindle away? Or maybe it would pick up. Patrons might hurry in to see the freak show. Kind of like passing an accident and stopping to stare.

Most troubling of all was her concern for Buddy's safety.

Either Clare Barker or Tony Weeden, maybe both, had come into their home last night. Laney shivered at the memory of that stick-figure drawing. Had the same person drawn the one left in Buddy's room and the ones on the motel wall? What kind of sick person did that? And what the hell was the idea behind marking them out?

She wasn't sure she could deal with the answer to that question right now.

As soon as the hardware store opened this morning, Hayden had changed the locks on the doors at the house. He'd ensured the locks on all the windows worked and he'd called a reputable security-monitoring company. Unfortunately they couldn't get her on their schedule until next week.

Meanwhile, Hayden was the protection. Warmth spread through her at the thought of having him near. She didn't usually let anyone this close but she hadn't had much of a choice and, if she were honest with herself, she would have to admit that it had been easier than she'd expected.

He was nice and seemed to genuinely care about her and Buddy. And her son loved him.

Buddy had never taken to anyone the way he'd latched on to Hayden.

Then again, that swiftly developing relationship was worrisome, as well. How would Buddy take it when Hayden went away? He was only here for work.

For that matter, how would *she* take it?

Apparently, having just met the guy wasn't going to deter that long-neglected romantic side of her that still existed. She'd thought that foolish part of every young woman's fantasy had died years ago. Had to be some renegade gene she'd inherited from her crazy biological parents.

She'd had those old nightmares last night. The ones she hadn't experienced since right after her parents—the only ones she'd ever known—had died in that awful car accident. The screaming… God, she hated the screaming. Children sobbing, a woman screaming and the darkness. That nightmare had haunted her for years. But it had gone away after Buddy was born. All she'd had to do was cuddle up with Buddy and Mr. Bear and she slept like a baby.

Didn't take a self-help talk-show host to tell her that the mental stress was re-creating those same feelings of fear and insecurity she'd suffered after her parents had died.

Laney shoved her hair behind her ears and tried to relax. She couldn't get worked up about any of that and expect to be coherent in this meeting. She'd dressed in her best jeans and most conservative and businesslike blouse. Her grandmother always said that there were two times in a person's life when they needed to look their best. When asking for a loan and when going to the doctor. As a kid, Laney had giggled and asked her grandmother why it mattered if you looked good for a doctor's appointment. Most folks only went to the doctor when they were sick anyway. Her grandmother had lifted an eyebrow and given her a nod before saying, "You want 'em to think you're worth saving, dear heart."

Good advice in Laney's opinion.

The gentleman with the appointment ahead of her exited the president's office.

Finally.

"Ms. Seagers."

Laney stood and rearranged the worry on her face into something she hoped was optimistic. "Mr. Teague."

"Let's have a seat in my office."

Laney followed, took the seat in front of his desk. Because he hadn't smiled or made more than fleeting eye contact with her, fear twisted in her belly.

"I understand you ordered our appraiser off your property." Still no eye contact. He focused on the file she presumed to be hers.

"I did." She steeled herself. "Since I didn't receive advance notice from your office, I wasn't sure if the gentleman was legit." He looked up then. "Allowing a stranger into my home is not a common policy of mine." She didn't need to remind him that she was a single woman with a small child. That was all in the file.

Mr. Teague heaved a big breath and leveled his gaze on her then. "Your profit and loss statements for the first quarter look very good, Laney. Last year's net profits gave you a strong year."

She nodded. "That's exactly why I don't see the problem with refinancing."

He sighed. "I'm going to be completely honest with you."

Fear kicked her heart against her sternum. "I appreciate that, sir."

"I don't have an issue with renewing your loan. You have gone above and beyond to show your credit worthiness. The collateral assets are in place. As an independent bank we're not as constrained as the larger banks when it comes to making loans. I do, however, have to answer to my board. Therein lies the problem."

"I always pay on time, Mr. Teague, and as you just said, I'm showing the necessary profit margin."

"All true." He closed the file and leaned back in his chair. "The board is made up of powerful businessmen who have stock in this bank. I am only one voice on that board. There are others who are considering the proposed loan renewal from a *different* view."

What the heck did that mean? "I don't understand." If her credit and her income were solid, what was the problem?

He looked away a moment, then seemed to come to a decision. "I'm taking a great risk in telling you this, but I feel you should know."

Laney braced for the worst.

"There is outside interference from a very influential man in Houston."

Terry's father. The bastard. Fury blasted her. "How can anything he say make a difference?"

"It shouldn't," Teague admitted, "but this is not a perfect world and, unfortunately, there are those who love nothing better than wielding their power."

"What am I supposed to do?" She squeezed the chair arms to keep herself seated. "My profit and loss statement for the year before last was a little in the red. You know the other bigger banks are going to need two solid years of strong profit for me to qualify."

"I have a friend at another independent bank," Teague offered. "I'm hoping he can help you. You have my word that I'm doing all I can."

Laney understood that he was unmistakably under tremendous pressure. She couldn't fault him and she sincerely appreciated him being honest with her.

"Thank you, sir." She stood, offered her hand across his desk.

"Don't give up on me."

Laney promised not to and left the bank feeling somewhat better about Teague and outright livid about Kingston. No wonder Teague had given her such a hard time last month. He'd been under major pressure himself.

Somehow she had to stop the Kingston family from trying to ruin all that she'd worked for.

Buddy deserved better.

5:15 p.m.

JOEL HESITATED IN THE HALL outside Laney's room. He hadn't meant to stumble into the part of voyeur but here he was and there she was.

She'd bent forward to brush all that honey-colored silk into a manageable bundle before securing it into a French twist that turned out all tousled and sexy instead of neat and serviceable. His gaze remained riveted to that cute bottom encased in worn denim. It wasn't until she straightened and reached for the hem of her blouse that he made a sound of warning. He cleared his throat.

Laney whipped around, jerked her T-shirt back down over that slim waist.

"Just wanted you to know the security system is up and running." And that his body was hard as a rock from merely looking at her.

"That was fast." She hugged her arms around her waist. "Thank you for pulling some strings or whatever you did to get them out here today."

He acknowledged her appreciation with a nod. He told himself to walk away but his need to stand right here and look at her and smell that subtle, sweet scent she wore held him prisoner. Hell, it was just lotion but, on her, it smelled soft and womanly and made him want to get closer.

She glanced around the room, visibly nervous or at a loss as to what to say next. Her attention locked on the window. "So those things on the windows will make the alarm go off if the glass is broken?"

When her gaze found his once more her eyes

were wide. She licked her lips, waiting for him to answer or to make a move. Too hard to tell— in more ways than one.

He crossed the room, drew back the curtain and pointed to the sensors. "These are for letting you know if anyone raises a window. If you forget to lock it for some reason or if the glass break fails and someone reaches inside and unlocks the window and attempts to raise it. There's a sensor on the ceiling at the other end of the hall that triggers the alarm if the distinct pitch of glass breaking is detected."

Laney nodded. "Oh. Well, good." She took a breath. "You'll show me how to arm and disarm the system?"

"It's simple." He moved back to the electronic keypad by her door. "You have two keypads. One here and one at the front door since that's the one you use most often."

He might have made it through this teaching session just fine if she hadn't moved in so close to watch. Forcing his attention on the keypad, he took her through the steps of arming and disarming, delayed and instant status.

"If you press these two buttons simultaneously, that's the panic mode. The police will be notified immediately. If the fire detectors have picked up any smoke or excessive heat, the fire department will be notified, as well."

"Man. I need something like that at the High Noon."

She definitely did. "I can see what kind of package deal they can offer for the two."

"Remember," she cautioned, "my budget's limited."

The silence thickened for several seconds. She waited for him to say something, he supposed. But his mind wasn't on talking at the moment. The electricity zinging between them was burning him up. Moving away from that hypnotizing pull was out of the question. If they were lucky she would break the spell with a word or gesture...anything.

Finally she looked up at him. "I never get involved with employees." The need blazing in her eyes protested the statement.

"Technically, I'm not an employee." His voice was husky and there wasn't a damned thing he could do about that. He wanted to touch her but didn't dare. He, too, had a rule against getting involved with a client...but technically she wasn't his client.

"Guess not," she agreed. She licked those lush lips again. "Truth is, I haven't been kissed in more than three years. I may have forgotten how it's done."

He reached out and removed the clip that held her hair. Joel had been dying to touch that silky mane since the first time he laid eyes on her. He threaded his fingers into the mass and massaged the back of her neck.

She trembled. "I'm usually a lot more cautious than this."

He lifted his other hand and traced the soft contour of her cheek. She was a beautiful woman but she didn't seem to have a clue. Wide brown eyes. Lush lips set in a creamy complexion. Even her nose was cute.

"Caution is good," he murmured. "You're a beautiful woman, Laney. You work hard. You deserve a man who'll treat you right."

"I know you'll be leaving when this is over." She leaned into his hand. "But," she said as she searched his eyes, "I have this feeling that if I hold back with you, I'll regret it for the rest of my life. I already have enough regrets."

He leaned down, brushed his lips against hers and she trembled again. He kissed her slowly, tenderly, the way a man should kiss this kind of woman. She'd been treated badly, neglected and thrown away. He wanted her to know that it wasn't always like that. He wanted her to feel what a kiss from the right man felt like.

Her arms went around his neck and he slid his hands down her back and pulled her close. She made the sweetest sound as her quivering body formed to his as if they were made to fit together. She tasted like the peach she'd eaten a few minutes ago, soft and ripe with need.

He wanted to strip those clothes off her and make love to her right now but they had to be at the saloon in an hour and though Buddy was occupied for the moment with his new building set, he was awake and that made the option unacceptable.

She drew her lips from his and pressed her forehead to his chin. "That was really nice." She toyed with the collar of his shirt. "I hope I didn't scare you off with my neediness."

He lifted her face to his and looked directly into her eyes. "That was very nice. And I don't think you needed that any more than I did."

She backed up, managed a smile. "I have to get ready to go." She gestured to the High Noon T-shirt lying on the bed.

Joel gave her a smile and decided a walk was in order.

Maybe a long walk.

Chapter Twelve

Wednesday, May 29th, 7:45 a.m.

Heat glided along her body…made her sweat. Laney curled deeper into the warmth. She didn't want to wake up…. She wanted this to last. To feel his body tangled with hers for just a little while longer.

Stranger. She ignored the voice. Yes, he was a stranger but she needed to trust him. She could trust him. Her mind grew dark and darker still…. Where was he? She felt cold, alone. The screaming wouldn't stop.

Mommy!

She held her bear tighter and squeezed her eyes shut tight. *Please make it stop!*

Mommy!

I'm here, sweet girl…. Mommy's here.

"Mommy!"

Laney's body quaked. She tried to open her eyes, but the darkness wouldn't let go.

"Mommy, wake up!"

The shaking started again. Her eyelids lifted, fluttered. The light was bright. Too bright.

"Come on, sleepyhead."

Laney came fully awake and found her boy perched on the edge of her bed shaking her again. "Morning, Buddy."

"You have to get up!" He jumped off the bed and rushed over to the window. "Mr. Joel is on the barn roof but he won't let me play up there with him."

Laney threw the covers back and climbed out of the bed. She stared at the clock in disbelief. Almost eight o'clock. Good Lord, she never slept that late.

She slid her feet into her house slippers. "I'm sorry, baby, you must be starving."

"We ate already." Buddy rushed over and grabbed her hand to tug her to the window. "I need to help Mr. Joel."

Laney stood at the window and stared across her backyard. Hayden was on the roof of the old barn nailing down the loose tin. The sun glistened on his bare back. The feel of his lips moving over hers had her body growing warm. They'd barely skirted a repeat performance after she'd put Buddy to bed last night.

She'd wanted more. Oh, how she had wanted more. But she had known that she would never be able to stop with a kiss. No way. His body felt so strong when he'd held her against him. Strong and powerful and somehow humble and gentle.

The way his jeans fit his body made her want to explore every part of him over and over until she knew him by heart. She turned back to her bed where she'd curled into the covers leaving them a tangled mess. She'd dreamed of lying with him that way, their bodies connected completely.

But then that old, too-familiar nightmare had intruded. The screaming and the sobbing…and the bear. That was the first time she'd remembered the bear from the dream. She'd always sensed she'd been holding on to something in the dream.

Maybe it was symbolic.

"Mom-mee!"

"Okay, okay. Let me get dressed and make the bed."

"I make mine, too!"

Buddy dashed from the room. Moving slower than usual, Laney changed into jeans and a cami. She roamed a brush through her hair and watched Hayden. It was guilty pleasure but who would know?

He finished nailing down one section, scrubbed the sweat from his brow with his forearm and moved on to the next. Her gaze followed that bare torso down to his low-riding jeans. Even from across the yard the delineated, sinewy lines were enough to make her throat go dry.

"Snap out of it, Laney." *If you want him that badly, take him,* a wicked voice taunted.

But would that really be fair? Extreme stress wasn't a good reason to have sex. That was something two people should do in a relationship…a mutually beneficial relationship. Not this one-sided neediness.

What was wrong with her? She had worked hard to be an independent, self-reliant woman. Now this insanity from the past blows into town and suddenly she's all squishy and wishy-washy. Enough with the fantasy world.

Buddy was still fiddling with his bedcovers when she paused at this door. "Need some help?"

He dropped the corner of his quilt and sighed. "I think so. It won't cop'erate."

Laney smiled. What big words her boy used. "Okay. Let's see what we can do to get some cooperation."

As she tidied the linens and then the quilt, Buddy frowned. "What's wrong? You don't like the way I'm doing it?" This wouldn't be the first time her son had decided a task could be done better or a different way. His little mind worked a mile a minute.

"She wouldn't come inside," he said with another sigh. "I told her to but she didn't listen."

A chill slithered over Laney. "Who wouldn't come inside?"

He scrunched his face and looked up at his mom. "You know, the grandma lady."

The chill turned to fear. "Where did you see her?"

He pointed to his window. "Right there."

"When?" The word was brittle with the ice freezing her blood.

He shrugged. "Dark time."

Stay calm, Laney. If she scared him he might not get all the facts straight. "You woke up and saw her there? In the dark?" Maybe it was just a dream. He couldn't have seen her in the dark…maybe the moonlight. She couldn't remember if the moon had been particularly bright last night.

"The light woke me up." He picked up Mr. Bear and propped him on his pillow. "It shined in my face."

"What kind of light?" Laney sank to the bed, her knees too weak to keep her standing.

He puckered out his bottom lip and shrugged again. "I dunno. It was in my face and I woke up. Then it was on her face. I could see her there." He pointed to the window again. "I tried to open the window. It was too hard."

"Come here." Laney tried to control the way her body trembled so he wouldn't notice. She patted the bed. "Let's talk about the grandma lady a minute."

Buddy bounced up on the bed. "She's old."

Laney tried to smile. "Old to you."

Buddy smiled and gazed up at her. "Old to you, too."

She ruffled his hair. "I'll take that as a compliment." *Deep breath. Keep it low-key.* "This grandma lady is a stranger, Buddy. It's not safe to talk to strangers or to let them in our house. We've talked about strangers before."

He nodded emphatically. "But she's a grandma. Old people are nice."

Laney hugged her sweet son. "Sometimes they can be bad, too. We can't be fooled by how nice someone seems." God knew she had half a lifetime of experience with that one. Her gaze drifted beyond the window to where Hayden worked on the barn. Maybe she hadn't learned her lesson yet.

"You don't want me to be nice to her?"

Laney turned his face up to her and looked him in the eyes. He knew this was the listen-good signal. "You be nice to everyone, William Seagers. But you never, ever let yourself be alone with strangers. No matter how nice they look. You don't go anywhere with them and you don't let them get too close to you."

He nodded, his head moving up and down in her hands.

"If anyone, even the grandma lady, comes to your window or to the door again, you come and get me. Promise?"

"Promise. But she didn't say anything. She was just smiling at me."

More of that fear crowded into her throat. "And you're sure this wasn't a dream?"

He nodded. "After a while she turned off the light and then she was gone." He moved his shoulders up and down. "Least I couldn't see her no more."

"Just remember to come get me next time."

"I promise."

"Now." Laney gave him a hug. "Let's go see what's left of breakfast." She had to talk to Hayden but she didn't want to upset Buddy.

The woman had come back.

"Bacon," Buddy called out as they raced to the kitchen. "Biscuits." He skidded to a stop at the island. "But not your biscuits."

Laney laughed out loud when she saw the little mound of small, knotty biscuits. The scrambled eggs looked fine and the bacon nice and crisp. But the poor biscuits. She laughed some more. Buddy jumped up and down and laughed with her. Tears streamed from her eyes. Maybe the hysteria was more related to what Buddy had told her than the pitiful biscuits.

"What's so funny?"

Laney jumped. She'd been laughing so hard she hadn't heard the screen door. With her lips compressed to stifle the mirth, she attempted to compose herself.

"Mom was laughing at your biscuits!"

"Buddy!" Laney couldn't help it. She burst into laughter again. This time it sounded more like sobs.

Hayden searched her face as she once again struggled to compose herself.

When she could speak without the words jerking, she said, "Buddy, I'd like you to tidy the living room for me this morning. You know how."

"Okay." He lumbered off as if she'd just grounded him for a whole week.

When he was out of earshot, Hayden frowned. "What's wrong?"

Was the front door locked?

"Just a minute." Laney rushed to the front door and checked to ensure the screen was latched and the door was locked, dead bolt included.

By the time she returned to the kitchen she

had swiped her eyes and caught her breath. Hayden waited, his expression serious. He'd pulled his T-shirt back on and had his hands planted on his hips.

"A light woke Buddy last night." The idea that she had been asleep in her room just a few feet away and Hayden had been on the sofa stunned her. Did this woman have no fear? "Someone was at his window shining—" She shrugged. "I guess, shining a flashlight in his face to awaken him."

"Was it her?" Fury simmered in his tone.

Laney nodded, tears welling once more. "She shined the light on her face so he could see that it was her."

"Did she talk to him?"

"No. He said she just stared at him for a while and then left." Laney hugged herself. "What does she want?"

Hayden closed in, pulled her into his arms. "I wish I knew. Until we find her, we can't take any chances. I'll add motion sensors to the exterior lights. That way she won't have the cover of darkness."

Laney closed her eyes and tried to block all the worries with the feel of his strong body and that scent of clean, sun-kissed sweat. As much as she wanted to be strong and take care of Buddy and herself on her own, she knew she could not do this alone.

He drew back, then ushered her to a stool. "Sit. Eat. When you've had a minute to relax, we'll look around outside and I'll give Lucas an update."

She poured herself a cup of coffee while he readied her plate. Prepared for the worst, she nibbled on one of the biscuits that looked more like a stubby dinosaur egg. To her surprise it was good.

"Not as bad as you thought, huh?"

She rolled her eyes. "Not as bad as I thought. Actually they're pretty good." She concentrated to pinpoint the flavors. "Garlic and cheese. Really nice."

He slid onto a stool and smiled at her from across the old wooden countertop. "When you've been a bachelor as long as me, you have to learn to whip up a few things."

She realized there was a lot more she didn't know about him. "How old are you?"

"My thirty-fifth birthday is in December."

"Wow." She made a face. "You're like an old maid except you're a guy."

He scowled. "Funny."

"You always lived in Houston?"

"Grew up in Galveston. Most of my family

still lives there." He plucked a biscuit from the bowl and tore off a bite.

Laney got distracted for a moment by his mouth. She blinked. "I find it hard to believe you've never even gotten close to marriage." A guy this good-looking, nice, great job... He was a catch.

"Let's just say I went through a long *me* stage," he confessed. "I wasn't interested in complications. I was focused on my career and having a good time."

"Aha." She sipped her coffee. Not quite as good as her own, but close. "You were a player. A heartbreaker."

He grinned. "I guess I was."

"What changed?" Obviously something had. Since it wasn't first love or a wedding or a child, it had to be a significant event. Her pulse rate slowly returned to normal. As normal as possible considering just being in the room with him seemed to have some impact on her ability to breathe.

Under normal circumstances she would chastise herself for going off into romantic fantasyland, but right now she desperately needed an escape. Tension started to knot in her belly. *Don't think about it. Not yet.* It was all still too painful and overwhelming.

All that mattered was that Buddy was safe.

As his mother, whatever was required to keep him that way was her job. But she was only human. Finding a little relief—even if only in a moment of romantic fantasy—was not such a bad thing.

Hayden seemed lost in thought for a moment, as if trying to decide if he wanted to remember whatever had made him take a step back and assess his life.

"My older brother—they're all married." He laughed softly. "But he married the one woman for him. High-school sweethearts. Bought the house with the picket fence, two kids and a dog. Life was perfect. Exactly what marriage and family should be. The kids came home from school one day and she was gone."

Laney felt her eyes widen in dismay. "She left?"

Hayden shook his head. "She had an undiagnosed heart defect. She finished the laundry that day, sat down to fold the towels and she was gone."

"That's just awful."

"Really awful." He turned to the fridge and helped himself to a bottle of water. One twist of the cap and he chugged down about half of it. "I watched him go through the stages of grief. The kids were devastated. His whole life fell apart for a little while. Then he sucked it up and did what he had to do."

"Did he eventually find someone else?" Laney decided this was about the saddest story she'd ever heard.

"There's someone now but it's a slow go." He deposited the bottle of water on the counter. "The point is I realized that the relationship between men and women—that kind of relationship—was too precious to treat with such insignificance. Hearts aren't meant to be broken. And I broke more than my share."

Now Laney was confused. "So, you avoid relationships altogether?" Exactly why she felt so intensely disappointed at the prospect escaped her at the moment.

"I'm cautious. I don't lead anyone on and I don't play games."

"That's a good thing," she offered, hoping that was the right thing to say. "People shouldn't play games with other people's lives." The way Terry was playing with hers and Buddy's.

Laney couldn't avoid the subject any longer. The fear was gnawing at her again. "What does this woman want from us?" Surely she didn't expect herself or the others to see her as their mother. Dear God, the thought was unbearable.

"That's the problem." He braced his hands

wide apart on the counter and showed with his eyes that he was dead serious. "If Rafe Barker is right, Clare is a killer. If he's straight-up lying, she falls somewhere between accomplice and victim. Either away, she has an agenda. And until we know what that agenda is, none of you are safe."

"What about this man who's with her? The one-armed man?" As much as she hated to prejudge, this whole thing felt like something from a horror flick.

"We haven't confirmed the suspicion, but we believe Tony Weeden is Clare's son from her college days. She may have been raped by a professor. We don't know how the two reunited. Maybe Weeden learned the identities of his biological parents and sought them out. We can't be sure."

Laney thought of the two people who had raised her until their untimely deaths. William and Lana Seagers were her parents. Her grandma Seagers had been her most beloved companion. She took care of Laney whenever her parents were away on business. It was her grandma's heart attack that had her parents rushing home. Her grandmother had died in the hospital that night. Before dawn, her parents had been killed in the crash.

And she had been left all alone.

Laney pushed the memories away. "Do you really believe the Colby Agency can find the truth in time?"

"To save Rafe Barker in the event he's innocent?"

Laney nodded. That man was her biological father. Was he a monster or a victim? Had he sacrificed his life to save his daughters?

"If anyone can," Hayden promised her, "the Colby Agency can."

The implications of how this changed her life were only just now setting in. But then again, once Clare was stopped was there any reason for anything to change?

"Let's have a look outside Buddy's window."

Laney followed him outside. Despite the sun, she felt cold. She wrapped her arms around herself.

The window was certainly low enough to the ground for someone to be able to climb in were it open. She prayed her talk with Buddy would prevent him from viewing this woman with curiosity. He needed to be afraid of her.

Hayden examined the window carefully. Then he surveyed the ground nearby. Laney followed as he walked all the way around the house. He made a call to Lucas and told him about the incident. Lucas had no news.

The search for Clare was getting nowhere.

Hayden found nothing in the yard. It hadn't rained recently so there were no footprints. And no forgotten evidence.

Buddy's description had been far too vivid to have been a dream. Of that she felt confident. The woman had been here.

At the back door, he hesitated. "Maybe it would be better if Buddy slept in the room with you until this is done."

Laney had been thinking the same thing. "He won't like it. He's a big boy now, you know."

"Maybe we can convince him of how lumpy that sofa is and that I really need a bed to sleep in. Or that you're afraid to sleep alone."

Hayden and bed in the same thought gave her another little shiver but it had nothing to do with fear. "He'd probably go for that."

He hesitated again before opening the door. There was something in his eyes that held her still. Warmed her through and through.

"I'd rather be in your bed," he said, his voice thick with desire. "But your safety comes first."

As if he'd just told her the sky was blue, he turned and walked into the house.

Laney stayed back a minute. She needed a moment to compose herself. For a guy who had given up the player lifestyle, he sure knew how to reel a woman in.

Careful, Laney, don't get in over your head. A few days or weeks from now and he'll be long gone.

She'd had her heart broken too many times already.

When she wandered through the house in search of the man who had somehow banished her discipline in a short enough period to be measured more accurately in hours than days, he unknowingly delivered another blow to her defenses.

Hayden had sprawled on the floor to play Legos with Buddy. Maybe the sight wouldn't have disarmed her so had Hayden not been having a blast with her son.

She'd made a mistake letting him so close. Now she and Buddy would both pay.

Chapter Thirteen

Thursday, May 30th, 1:40 a.m.

Joel lifted Buddy from the car seat in the backseat of his Jeep. He'd checked the perimeter of the yard, then the house to ensure there were no surprises. With the security system in place he wasn't anticipating any surprises inside.

Laney gathered the kid's toys and bear and followed. She was exhausted. The meeting had gone well at the bank that morning and the crowd had been heavy and happy at the saloon tonight—both good things. But she was beat, emotionally and physically.

Two nights in a row without an appearance by Kingston was another good thing. Unless the jerk was up to something that would open a whole new can of worms for Laney. Joel didn't want any more trouble with the guy but if he showed up intending to give Laney a hard time, trouble was what he would get.

In the house, Laney drew the covers back on her bed and Joel settled Buddy there. Once the covers and his stuffed bear were tucked in, Laney gave her boy a kiss and moved quietly out of the room.

Joel almost hated to go. Her scent permeated the air of her private space. That sweet lotion she wore and that natural, womanly scent drove him mad with desire. From the old iron headboard to the whitewashed wood nightstand, the whole room was her. She had a distinctive flare and he liked that about her. He honestly could not recall ever having paid attention to a woman's taste in decorating.

He hadn't meant for this to happen. This insatiable need to be close to her, to touch and taste her all over, was a strategic error but he couldn't change that now. She was so deep under his skin he wasn't sure there was any hope of backing up now.

Four days being this close and a few before that watching from a distance and he was hooked on the lady.

She was the first woman he'd bared his soul to when it came to his brother's tragedy and his own mistakes. Oddly, he didn't regret going there. He felt good about sharing that with her. It was his job to know everything about her, and somehow giving her something in return felt right.

On all other levels, however, they barely knew each other. The prospects of a relationship were fifty-fifty at best. But he couldn't not want her. She made him wish for those simple things he'd overlooked before.

He joined her in the kitchen. "Would you like a beer?" She stood next to the fridge, that old butcher's table between them.

Laney was nervous. He suspected she had a similar war going on inside. She was attracted to him, too. Occasionally he caught her watching him. He heard the way her breath hitched when he got too close. The idea that she wanted him made him want her all the more.

But he also recognized that she was terrified of getting hurt again. The last thing he wanted to do was hurt her.

She'd suffered too much of that already.

He held up a hand and declined her offer of a beer. "I'm good."

"Coffee?"

If she hadn't looked so hopeful he would have passed. "Your coffee? Anytime."

The smile that lit her face turned him inside out. He loved her smile. Tonight, behind that bar, she had been relaxed and in her element.

The folks loved her. She made the High Noon a fun and welcoming place to be.

With the loan worries lifted a little and her ex staying away, she didn't just serve her patrons, she performed a well-choreographed production of smooth moves and snappy dialogue. It was no wonder the High Noon was such a success.

The lady had a gift.

And his full attention.

Once she had the coffeemaker set, he moved up behind her and whispered in her ear, "I couldn't take my eyes off you tonight."

She turned to face him, trapped between his body and the counter. "I hope your boss didn't notice."

Lucas had stopped by for a few minutes. Then he'd gone back on the prowl for his prey. Clare Barker and Tony Weeden had seemingly fallen off the planet. Lucas was having no luck finding the first sign of the two in Beaumont.

"I think every male in the house tonight was watching you, my boss included."

She smiled, her lips trembling. "Is that one of your old player lines or is that a true compliment?"

So the lady needed some convincing, did she? Well, he was way past restraint. No matter that she was his principal and this was business, there was no going back. He was in this for the long haul.

He leaned down and nuzzled her neck, loving the feel of her silky hair against his jaw. He lavished her ear with his tongue then whispered, "You are so beautiful."

"It's been a long time," she murmured. "I'm not so sure this will be as easy to fall back into as kissing."

"We'll take it slow."

She searched his eyes. He showed her with his that she had nothing to fear from him. That he wanted her so, so much. He recognized the moment she made her decision. The worry that had furrowed her brow eased away. Her gaze drifted down to his mouth. He kissed her, softly, slowly. His body reacted instantly, hardening with the need to show her just how beautiful it could be between a man and a woman. He wanted her to know that beauty. To feel all those other emotions and sensations beyond simple lust and desire.

She sidled out of his reach and hurried into the hall. He trailed after her. She made a stop at the linen closet and retrieved a big colorful quilt. She glanced back at him in invitation and he followed her to the living room. He liked following Laney. The view never got boring.

She spread the quilt on the floor. Its once-

vibrant hues of red and blue were faded with
time. She toed off her boots, rolled off her
socks and clicked off the table lamp, leaving
nothing but the moonlight filtering in through
the windows to guide their way. There was the
slightest tremor in her movements. As much as
she wanted this, she was still nervous.

He removed his boots and socks, then
reached for the clip from her hair and threaded
his fingers through that luxurious mane. After
tossing the clip aside, he tugged her T-shirt
from the waistband of her jeans and peeled
it off her slim torso. He had to look at her a
moment before continuing. Her body was perfect. Tall, lean but with a nice slender hour-
glass shape.

She reached behind her and unfastened her
bra, allowing it to fall away as he watched. His
breath stalled in his lungs as he took in her
creamy, high breasts. He reached out, closed
his hands over those lush mounds. She gasped.
He massaged her breasts, paying special attention to her taut nipples. Then he let his hands
glide up her shoulders and gave the same treat-
ment there. Her shoulders and arms were likely
tired from making and serving drinks all night.
He wanted her completely relaxed. He wanted
her to enjoy every moment of this special time
between them.

With prompting she turned her back to him and he lavished her neck and upper back with just the right rubbing and squeezing and soft pressure with his fingers. By the time he finished she was moaning with his every touch. He moved his body up against hers, loving the feel of her bottom nestled against his pelvis. With his arms around her, he released the fly of her jeans, but instead of pushing them down, he reached inside and found that hot, damp spot that made her whimper with need. He stroked and teased until she quivered in his arms, her screams of pleasure barely restrained.

He turned her around to face him and he dropped to his knees. First he kissed each breast, nipped at her nipples, then he slid those tight-fitting jeans down and off.

Slowly, he kissed every part of her. He traced her ribs with his tongue and explored her bellybutton while he kneaded her bottom with his hands. Her fingers fisted in his hair and she quivered with the pleasure building inside her. He restrained his own, refused to give in to the urgency until he made sure this was worth the wait for her. Three years was a long time to wait.

When her breathing became more and more frantic, he slid a hand between her trembling thighs and stroked her some more. Her hips undulated with his movements and then her body tensed. He felt the waves of completion crashing down on her, her inner muscles flexing and contracting around his fingers.

He had to have her soon.

He stood and began to unbutton his shirt.

She opened her eyes and stared for a long moment, watching his methodical movements. Then she came at him.

EMBOLDENED FROM A powerful orgasm, Laney ripped his shirt from his body. She would buy him a new one. Right now she just needed him naked so she could feel his hot skin. She clawed at his belt and fly until they were open. As still as stone and every bit as hard, he watched her every frantic move with an intensity that made her shiver. She wanted him to watch. But more importantly, she wanted to do to him what he had just done to her. She dragged off his jeans. She sat back on her heels and stared at his naked body. He looked amazing. Strong, lean lines. Sculpted muscles. Perfect. She leaned in, inhaled deeply of his masculine scent, then she started to lick. She teased him with her mouth and tongue until he trembled. He tangled his fingers in her hair, begged her to slow down. When she felt him start to throb she drew away. He was heavy with need and she wanted that weight inside her.

Laney fell back onto the quilt she had inherited from her grandmother and opened herself to him. He came down on top of her and filled her in one forceful thrust. She climaxed instantly. His body shook with restraint as he brought her once more to that place. He urged her on until, their bodies shuddering, they found release together.

He rolled onto his side and held her, their bodies still entwined. She snuggled against his chest and listened to the frantic sound of his heart beating. She felt sated and safe.

Eventually she would need to shower and pull on a gown so that she could go to her room and snuggle up to her son. But for now she wanted to be held just like this.

He stroked her hair, kissed her forehead and cheek. She couldn't be sure but she sensed that their lovemaking had affected him as deeply as it had her. She hoped so.

He tipped her chin up to look in her eyes. "You okay?"

She smiled. "I'm better than okay." The truth was no one had ever made love to her like that.

"Yes, you are."

Tears burned in her eyes and she wanted to kick herself for getting all weepy but there was no stopping it. He had made her feel special and she'd needed that so much.

He caressed her cheek. "I don't know about you but I think an early breakfast is in order."

"As long as I get to make the biscuits."

He laughed. "I figure that's a good idea."

They helped each other dress, kissing over and over again. Her lips would be bruised tomorrow, he had kissed her so many times. She decided to forego her jeans, and rushed off to the kitchen in her T-shirt and panties. That she didn't feel the need to cover herself completely in his presence with the lights on was new for her. She'd had a baby and had the marks to prove it. The proof of motherhood hadn't bothered him.

In the kitchen, he was in charge of the eggs and she made the biscuits the way her grandmother had taught her. It felt real, it felt right. Every move was accompanied by a smile or a kiss.

When the biscuits were in the oven, he sat her on the counter and kissed her some more. Each time was somehow different from the last. The way he cradled her face or touched his tongue to hers. Then he lifted her T-shirt to admire her breasts.

He leaned her back against the cabinets. She arched her back, forcing her breasts to jut upward. He explored each one with his fingers and then his mouth.

She tried to hold back from losing herself to his touch, but she couldn't. He had her on the brink of release all over again. He lifted her into his arms and she wrapped her legs around his waist. He fumbled with his zipper until he was free, then, pushing her panties aside, he guided her down onto his erection.

He lifted her over and over, each time letting her slide down that rigid length until they both moaned with release.

Moments later, without even setting her down, he turned off the oven and carried her to the bathroom. They made love again in the shower. Afterwards, he washed her body and she washed his. She learned every part of him. They toweled each other off, went their separate ways to dress and rendezvoused in the kitchen for soggy eggs and hard biscuits.

"Your coffee is amazing," he said after finishing off his cup.

She kissed him and smiled. "One of these days I plan to serve breakfast at the saloon." She loved to cook and she had imagined making beautiful pastries and gourmet omelets to go with the unique blends of coffee she would offer.

"I think that's a brilliant idea." He pulled her

against him and settled onto a stool with her in his lap. "You'd need a much bigger staff. Your location is perfect for those morning commuters on the long drive to Houston."

It pleased her immensely that he thought her plan was a good one. "I want to keep the western theme but give it a slight sophisticated quality for morning hours."

"With those biscuits and that coffee, it's a sure success."

"Then maybe I can find the right person to manage the place at night so I can spend more time at home with Buddy."

They talked for a long time about her plans and how she could make those dreams come true. At some point she fell asleep, but was roused as he tucked her into her bed next to Buddy. He smiled down at her and her lips immediately responded.

"Good night." He brushed a kiss across her cheek.

"Night."

When he would have turned away she caught his hand. He stared down at her and her breath left her at how handsome he was. A fact she had noticed over and over since he'd first swaggered into the High Noon.

She peered up into his eyes. "Thank you

for protecting us and for making me feel alive again."

He squeezed her hand and smiled before walking away.

Her last thought before she drifted off was of him and how much she wanted this to be real…not just a dream.

Chapter Fourteen

2:00 a.m.

Clare watched longingly as the last of the lights went out in Lisa's home. The man from the Colby Agency had seduced her. Even from the road Clare had been able to see them come together before the lights went out in the living room. Two vague forms falling into each other's arms. She had known that kind of desperation once.

But it had been a mistake.... Except for the three beautiful daughters that had come of that tainted marriage. Fury and misery stormed inside her. She wanted him and all who had helped him to pay for stealing her life.... For taking her babies.

For ruining everything.

Soon they would all know the truth.

No one could stop her now.

"We should take the boy."

Clare turned to her son. "He's beautiful, isn't he?"

Though she couldn't see Tony's fury in the darkness, she could feel the creeping thickness of it. He was angry for her. No one else save him understood what she had been through.... What she had lost.

For years she had sacrificed so much to keep *him* happy. And he had turned on her, used his silence to make her appear the guiltiest one.

Now he was only three weeks from being a dead man.

Joy shimmered through her. She closed her eyes and prayed that the devil would take him straight to hell.

"We should take him," Tony repeated.

Clare shook off the wonderful thoughts of her husband burning for all of eternity and turned to her son. "He is very smart, too." Perhaps if she ignored Tony's comments he would let the idea go.

"She's a whore."

Clare surveyed the dark house, the turmoil inside her taking on a sharper edge. "She's a good mother." Clare had been a good mother to her daughters...but not to her son.

She had expected him to want to punish her

for what she had done so long ago. Instead, he had offered to help. He had prepared for her release and had welcomed her with open arms. She did not deserve his forgiveness.

"Is she a good mother?"

Tension coiled through Clare's body. "She is." Perhaps her son had decided she needed to be punished after all. "She was stronger than me. She kept her son and raised him despite having no one to help."

"She was not raped," Tony rebutted.

Clare wished she could see his eyes. This was the first time they had discussed that part of the past. Had he truly forgiven her? "I was young. Terrified and alone. I didn't know what to do." Though most of her life was a lie, that was the God's truth.

"You had *her*."

Rage rose to an instant boil. Her sister. Janet had done nothing but hurt her since the day Clare was born. She had learned the truth about her sister. But by then it had been too late. The damage was done.

Tony had paid a heavy price.

Clare had, as well. But now they would have their revenge on them all.

Rafe thought he had won by hiring this illustrious agency to help him. But he had not. Far from it. She was here. She had touched their grandson. She had seen all three of their beautiful daughters.

He would not win. Clare hoped he was afraid. That he lay in that tiny cell at night and wept at the idea that she was free and could do whatever she pleased. There was nothing he could do to stop her the way he had last time.

He was helpless, just as she had been twenty-two years ago. She had trusted him just as she had trusted her sister.

If only dear Janet had realized the error of her ways and run, she might still be alive. But she had remained, steadfast in her certainty that no one would see her lies.

She had gotten what was coming to her, though Clare doubted she had suffered nearly enough. She, too, would burn in hell.

"Yes," Clare said finally in response to her son's comment. "I had my sister." Again Clare wished she could see his face more clearly. "And look what she did to us." She touched his right shoulder. Agony twisted inside her.

"It was my fault."

How could he say that? He'd been a mere child when the accident happened. "She should have been watching you more closely." How could he blame himself?

"She was working and I got in the way."

Tony had told her that Janet had been chopping wood and he'd wanted to help. But Clare sensed that there was more he wasn't telling her. If he told her she would only feel more guilt. He suspected as much and wanted to shield her from it.

What a sweet man he had grown into despite what Clare had done to him. She should have kept him. What good had it done her to return to college and finish her degree?

None.

She had left Tony with Janet with the intention of coming back for him when she could support him. But then she had met Rafe and everything had changed.

Rafe had seemed such a deeply religious man she hadn't dared to tell him about the rape and her illegitimate son. Then she'd fallen so madly in love that she could see nothing but Rafe and the life he offered.

Janet hadn't spoken to her again for years. She had taken Tony away and Clare had been relieved.

Now she had the opportunity to make all of it right. All her past sins would be assuaged.

She sent one last longing look toward her daughter's home. Lisa had done all this on her own. She had been far smarter than her mother. Far stronger. Sarah was the same. Strong, hardworking. Clare had not located Olivia yet, but she was not giving up.

Soon they would all be together for the finale.

"We should go now," she said to Tony.

Ever obedient, he started the car and drove away. He waited a safe distance before turning on the headlights.

Clare sighed. Her plan was coming together, bit by bit.

She would not fail.

"We're being followed."

Clare jerked around to stare at the headlights far behind them. "Are you sure?"

"Yes," Tony insisted. "It's that man who has been looking for us all over town. The one from Copperas Cove."

Another from the Colby Agency. Lucas Camp. Clare knew they were trying to stop her.

Fury tightened her lips. She would stop their meddling. Didn't they realize they were working for the devil himself?

"Make sure you lose him."

Tony floored the accelerator, and the car leaped forward. "We need to be rid of him for good."

Clare said nothing. Just a few more days… and it would be done.

Chapter Fifteen

Lucas accelerated. Clare Barker would not elude him this time. He had her in his crosshairs.

The road wound through the countryside that separated Laney's home from the city of Beaumont for some fifteen miles. At this hour he should have no trouble staying on their tail even once they hit the city limits. Traffic would be negligible.

He had known Clare wouldn't be able to resist returning to watch Laney. The new security system had prevented her from getting too close to the house. Instead she and her accomplice had parked on the side of the road and watched from a distance.

And Lucas had been waiting.

The white sedan took a hard right, the vehicle nearly spinning a hundred and eighty degrees before barreling down this new side road.

Lucas made the same turn, his rented sedan

fishtailing with the change in momentum, tires screaming in protest.

He wrestled the steering wheel and forced the accelerator to the floor. The car lunged forward, gaining on his mark.

Victoria would be furious at his hazardous driving. But he could not lose Clare again. She'd gotten far too close to Laney and her son and that was on Lucas.

Another sharp turn, this one to the left. Lucas rode out the precarious maneuver, the smell of burning rubber accompanying the squealing tires.

Weeden appeared to be leading him deeper into the less populated countryside. Lucas wasn't worried. He was armed and ready. Let the bastard make a move.

The red warning of brake lights beamed in his face.

Lucas slammed on his brakes.

Weeden's car slid sideways on the road.

Lucas was going to collide with Weeden's car.

Heart pumping, Lucas cut to the right to avoid T-boning the vehicle.

The deep shoulder of the road threw Lucas's car into a tailspin. He struggled to regain control, but couldn't.

His car plunged off the road…down…down…

A tree stopped his forward momentum.

The air bag exploded, slamming into Lucas's body and forcing him against the seat.

An eerie silence was broken only by the ticking of the cooling engine.

One headlight shone on the trees in front of him.

Lucas gasped. The air bag had knocked the breath out of him. He tried to clear his head and take a mental inventory of any injuries he might have sustained.

His chest ached and…his left leg felt twisted or jammed somehow.

Phone. He reached for the console and fire shot through his right arm. He gritted his teeth against the pain and reached again. It wasn't there. Probably fell to the floorboard, he reasoned.

The sound of someone moving down the embankment on foot snapped Lucas to full attention.

It wouldn't be help… There was no one out here but Weeden and Clare Barker.

The pain making him growl with agony, he tried to get to the weapon in the shoulder holster he wore beneath his jacket. Sweat beaded on his forehead.

He couldn't do it. Damned right shoulder had to be dislocated.

He reached for the door handle with his left hand. Incredibly, the door flew open. Lucas hit the seat belt release and tried to scramble out of the car. Pain roared through him.

A shadow blocked the moonlight.

He looked up into the face of Tony Weeden. His arm was raised high above his head.

Before Lucas could react, something crashed down on his head.

The pain went away.

Chapter Sixteen

High Noon Saloon, 8:40 p.m.

Joel was worried. Lucas had not checked in with him all day. The last time they talked was when the High Noon closed up last night. When Joel and Laney arrived to set up for opening around five-thirty this evening there had been no sign of Lucas. No indication that he had slept in the office. His cell phone went straight to voice mail.

Lucas wouldn't just disappear and he certainly wouldn't fail to check in.

Simon and Victoria had been attempting to locate him, as well. Simon had put in a call to Lucas's cell carrier in hopes of learning at least his last known location, by finding out the last cell tower his phone had reached out to. It would take time to muddle through the necessary approvals and Joel sensed that time was short.

Lucas was in trouble.

With the end of the work week approaching, the crowd at the High Noon was thick and rowdy. Good for Laney's bottom line but not so good when Joel was distracted. A guy had to be thankful for small favors, however, and one really good thing was that Kingston hadn't returned.

Maybe he'd ended up in jail or his father had shipped him back off to rehab. The guy needed rehabilitating. For Buddy's sake if not his own.

Lucas had spent the entire day yesterday searching for Clare Barker and Tony Weeden. He'd hit all the motels and hotels his first day in town. Then he'd moved on to restaurants and delis. At the top of his priority list were the cheaper and more out-of-the-way places. He'd found nothing. Like Joel, the man was feeling a little desperate about the situation. But even desperation wouldn't throw a man like Lucas so far off his game.

Joel scrubbed his chin. The only way Lucas would stay out of touch this long was if he had found serious trouble. Simon and Victoria had known him far longer than Joel and the consensus was the same. At this point they had to assume that Lucas needed backup. The problem was no one knew where to look. By late afternoon Simon and Victoria had arrived in Beaumont and were laying out a search grid, with every member of the Colby Agency's Houston office contributing to the search. Backup from the Chicago office had arrived by nightfall. Among those who had arrived was Jim Colby, Victoria's son.

The police had been notified but there was little they could do with no place to start and no evidence of wrongdoing by Clare or her son.

Part of Joel wanted to be out there looking for the older man but he couldn't risk diverting his attention from Laney and Buddy. Damn, this case was growing more complicated and murky with each passing day.

His gaze settled on Laney behind the bar. Like last night, she was on her A game. The crowd was jovial and the money was pouring into the cash register.

No matter how hard he tried to fight it, every time he looked at her, he couldn't stop the images and sensations and sounds from the hours they had spent making love from echoing through his mind...from tensing his muscles with the need to cross the room and touch her.

She had opened completely to him and he had fallen in deep. As crazy as it sounded, considering the short period they had known each other, he now understood the stories his brothers had told him about finding their true loves.

Something grabs you and won't let go.

Joel had no idea what tomorrow held but he sure didn't want to spend it without Laney and Buddy in his life. Even the notion of never seeing them again made his gut twist. Laney had been hurt so badly he wasn't sure how she would see them moving forward. He hoped she would at least consider the idea of exploring this bond between them. For the first time in his life, Joel desperately wanted to have a real relationship. Laney and Buddy made him long for a family of his own.

Not to mention the way Joel had fallen for the kid. God, he loved his nieces and nephews and he'd do anything in the world for any or all of them. This tyke had stolen his heart from the get-go. Maybe that midlife crisis Jeep hadn't done the trick. Maybe there was no outmaneuvering the need to bond with the opposite sex and procreate. Oddly, the idea of having children of his own didn't scare him in the least.

Laney caught him looking and grinned. They'd had breakfast a second time this morning. Buddy had set the menu and helped with rolling out and cutting the fresh biscuits.

Joel's throat tightened. As if all these years of bachelorhood had suddenly grown too heavy and had to be shrugged off, he wondered what it would feel like to hold a child of his own. To feel the weight of his baby in his hands and know that for the rest of his life that tiny human would mean the world to him.

He gave himself a mental shake. *Stay focused, man.* Maybe he should check on Buddy. See how Tatum was holding up in the kitchen. The man had been prepping and cooking all afternoon and things hadn't slowed down since the last time Joel checked. It may be good for business, but Tatum was obviously going to need help in the kitchen if this pace continued.

Weaving through the crowd slowed Joel down. The bank certainly couldn't complain about this level of business. Somehow that situation had to work out for Laney. She had worked too hard to have it all yanked from under her. If the bank gave her any more trouble, maybe he'd just have to see what he could do to help. If she allowed it. Laney Seagers was one independent lady. And she damned sure knew how to bring him to his knees. The idea of being so vulnerable to a woman should feel intimidating but somehow it didn't. It felt right.

Buddy sat atop a stainless-steel table in the middle of the kitchen. An array of big pots hung on the rack above his head. The last time Joel popped in, Buddy had two big wooden spoons and was using the pots for drums. Now, a Lego village was taking shape under his careful attention.

"Hey, Buddy!" Joel gave the boy a gentle punch to the shoulder. "Looks like you've about got your village finished."

"I think we need a fire truck."

Joel grinned. "Oh, yeah? I'll have to see what I can do about that." He'd decided that he would be worse than all three of his brothers put together when it came to spoiling kids. All these years he'd shaken his head at the way they spoiled their own. Joel would be eating crow on that when the time came.

Slow down. He was already mapping out fatherhood and marriage wasn't even on the table.

Somehow Laney and Buddy made him seriously consider all those things. No, they made him *want* those things.

Buddy stuck his thumb to his chest. "I don't need a fire truck." He crossed his legs, his little cowboy boots scrubbing against the tabletop. "Uncle Tater does. He's trying to burn the place down."

The kitchen was thick with humidity and a heck of a lot warmer than the saloon, even with that crowd out there. "Maybe I'd better check on him."

Buddy nodded. "He's over'helmed."

From the looks of things, Buddy was right. Tatum had three deep fryers going and the grill was loaded down with hamburger patties, chicken breasts and piles of thinly shaved beef. The massive toaster oven was loaded down with buns and sandwich rolls. He had to hand it to the guy, he was organized.

"You got this under control?" Joel dared to ask even after the old sailor shot him a narrowed look.

"Does a cat have climbing gear?" He glanced at the wheel hanging in the window that separated the kitchen from the saloon. The wheel was full with tickets from the waiter and waitresses. "In five minutes that wheel will be empty. Five minutes after that it'll be full again. It's a good kind of cycle and I've got my system." He waved his hand at the grill.

Joel gave him a nod. "You're a better man than me."

Tatum grinned. "A better cook, for sure."

Joel checked the back door before heading back out to the saloon. Tatum paid no attention. He was too focused on the grill and the fryers. The oven took care of itself, it seemed. Put the bread in at one end, and it rolled out the other onto what looked like a baking sheet.

The saloon was packed now. So far no one

was looking for trouble. Joel hoped it stayed that way.

Because he couldn't help himself, he propped at the end of the bar to watch Laney in action. Tonight there were two other bartenders, both female, dressed in the staff garb of a High Noon T-shirt, blue jeans and boots. One hustled between tending bar and waiting tables, depending upon which side of the bar was the furthest behind.

Laney had been going full speed for the past two hours. But Joel had watched her for more than a week now. The woman didn't take breaks until the last customer was happily served.

One of the other bartenders strolled up to him. "You need a drink, Hayden?" Her eyes glittered with a big smile stretched across her shiny lips. The lady was a flirt. But then, flirts and amateur psychologists made the best bartenders.

"No, thanks." He gave the lady a smile. She sashayed away, hoping to impress him with her practiced walk. Didn't work. He only had eyes for one woman.

He watched Laney a minute longer. Long enough for her to toss him one of those smiles that tugged on his heartstrings and then he wandered out into the crowd.

Near the swinging doors two men and a woman appeared to be having a strained discussion. Joel changed directions and headed that way. The lady stormed outside and one of the men followed. The other filtered back into the crowd.

Maybe not a good sign. Joel lingered at the door watching the couple. The woman slapped the man; he crushed her against his car.

Well, hell.

Joel strode toward the two, reached his destination just in time to snag the fool's arm before he slapped the blonde. "I don't think so, pal." He whipped the guy around and shoved him back. "Time for you to go home or to jail. Take your pick."

Behind him the woman took off. Good for her.

"That bitch started it," the guy bellowed. "She offered me her services for twenty bucks and then she tried to drag another guy into it to double her money."

"Whatever she offered you," Joel warned, "you don't hit a woman. You walk away."

"Whatever. I'm out of here."

Joel watched until the hothead had climbed into his truck. Across the lot a snazzy sports car peeled out onto the highway. Some folks just didn't have the sense to enjoy leisure time safely. That kind of behavior got innocent people killed.

A frown tugged at his brow when the blonde started ranting. What the hell was she doing now? She stood at the edge of the lot, evidently shouting at someone who had already driven away. Joel headed in that direction. The sports car was the only one to leave in the last couple of minutes. The truck driven by the guy who'd argued with the blonde peeled out next but the blonde appeared to pay no mind to him.

"What's the problem now, ma'am?"

She whipped around, her eyes wide and wild with something like fear. This was the first good look he'd gotten of her face. She looked familiar....

Damn. "You're the one who showed up with Kingston," he accused. The sports car that had hauled ass out of the lot flashed in his mind again. Not the vehicle Laney had taken the Louisville Slugger to, but a car along those lines.

She started to back away. "I had nothing to do with it. I just did what he told me." She glared at the highway. "Then the bastard drives away without me." A cold, hard reality rammed Joel right between the eyes.

Kingston had been here.

LANEY DEPOSITED THE two cold longneck bottles of beer onto the counter. "Enjoy, gentlemen."

The night's take was on the way to exceeding even the best of her Friday or Saturday nights. Hot damn. She wiped the bar where the two patrons had moved on to a table. With Mr. Teague offering to help and business booming, things were looking up.

Her hands slowed in their cleanup work and she smiled to herself. Things were looking up at home, too. As terrified as she was of getting her heart broken again, she had decided that Hayden was worth the risk.

Joel, she reminded herself. She'd promised to call him Joel from last night on. Seemed only right. When a woman knew a man that intimately, first names were a given.

Her body quivered with remembered desire as snippets of all the times and ways they had made love flashed through her head. No one had ever made love to her like that. As incredible as it had been, it had felt natural and right, as well. No regrets come dawn. Just the relentless desire for more.

Maybe tonight. She trembled at the idea.

Okay, Laney. Don't go falling head over heels after one night.

Giving herself a swift mental kick in the seat of the pants, she turned to go to the kitchen and check on Buddy. It hadn't been ten minutes but—

Smoke rolled from the serving window.

Smoke detectors started to wail.

Laney rushed toward the kitchen door. Tatum burst through the door, almost colliding head-on with her.

"That son of a bitch!" Tatum coughed, his face red as a beet. "He took Buddy. I couldn't stop him. He had a gun."

Laney pushed past him. The kitchen was thick with smoke. "Buddy!"

The back door was open, allowing the smoke to drift out of the room.

Laney's heart sank.

Buddy's Lego village was scattered on the table and floor.

She ran out the back door.

He was gone.

The narrow alley behind the building was vacant save for Tatum's old truck and the Dumpster.

Inside, panicked voices shouted… The music died… But Laney couldn't move.

Her baby was gone.

11:55 p.m.

JOEL WANTED TO KILL Terry Kingston. Not once had he ever really wanted to take another man's life until now.

The bastard didn't deserve to live.

The saloon had been cleared, thankfully without injury. The fire department and police had arrived. Two uniforms and an evidence tech had scoured the parking area and the kitchen. For all the good it would do.

The blonde, whose name was Margo Rucker, was being interrogated by the police. Margo couldn't give the license-plate number of the rental Terry had been driving, but she had helped complete the description Joel had gotten when the car spun out of the parking lot. An Amber Alert had been issued for Buddy.

The ache that accompanied that last thought made breathing impossible. He had to find that child. If Kingston got him hurt, Joel would kill the son of a bitch.

Laney was a mess. She paced back and forth in front of the office, furious the police wouldn't let her at the woman and terrified for her baby.

She wouldn't let Joel comfort her or even touch her for that matter.

Tatum had fallen completely apart. He might be a big bad ex-sailor but he was also a father and a grandfather. The guy sat on a bar stool, his head down. The rest of the staff had been interviewed by Joel and the police and then sent home.

Joel's cell vibrated. He dragged it from his pocket. Simon Ruhl. He hoped this was good news for a change. In the last update he'd gotten Lucas was still missing.

"Hayden," Joel said by way of greeting.

"Anything new on Buddy?" Simon asked.

Joel forked a hand through his hair. He wished he had better news to report. "The woman, Margo, said Kingston had spent the past two days coming up with this plan. She has no idea, she claims, where he was going from here. Houston PD has sent a couple of detectives to interview his father."

Luck had, unfortunately, been on Kingston's side tonight. Though he'd arranged for Margo to distract Joel, he hadn't anticipated the rear entrance being locked. But then the toaster oven had jammed and a fire had started. Tatum had put it out easily and quickly, but then he'd opened the back door to let out some of the smoke. Kingston had seized the opportunity. Margo had gotten the text message to "go" the instant Kingston had a way in.

Low-down dirtbag. If he got that boy hurt...

Margo had further stated that Kingston had been drinking but she'd seen him far drunker. Hopefully that was good news. Joel hadn't mentioned to Laney that the guy had roared away from the parking lot like a bat out of hell.

"I put in a call to Houston PD and asked that they put their finest on it," Simon assured him. "How is Laney holding up?"

"About as well as can be expected." Damn Terry Kingston. How could he use his son this way? Was the guy totally heartless?

"Keep her close, Hayden," Simon warned. "Her emotional state could prove a danger to herself and her son. We don't know what Clare Barker and Weeden have planned. It's doubtful Kingston's actions are related to their intentions but there are no certainties here."

"Got it covered." Christ. Joel hadn't even asked about Lucas. "What about Lucas? Any luck with the search?"

"His cell carrier has narrowed down his last registered location as being in the vicinity of Laney's home. Service is sketchy on some of the back roads between her house and the city. They can't pinpoint the area as well as we'd like but at least we have some place to search."

"His intent had been to stay at the High Noon," Joel said, mentally replaying his last conversation with Lucas. "If he changed his mind and decided to stake out the house, he never mentioned it."

"If Lucas had reason to suspect Clare and her accomplice would show up at Laney's home, he would follow that hunch."

"It would help if he'd given me a heads-up." The idea that he and Laney had spent hours making love while Lucas ran into trouble pained him deeply. Joel should have been providing backup instead of indulging in his own selfish needs.

"Lucas has spent a lifetime in covert operations. He's accustomed to following his instincts with or without backup. This was his decision. Bear that in mind."

That fact didn't relieve the regret Joel felt for not anticipating that kind of move out of a man like Lucas. As true as that was, he couldn't regret the bond he and Laney had formed.

Simon ended the call with the assurance he would keep Joel posted and Joel was to do the same.

The office door opened and the two detectives exited. Laney stalled in her pacing and waited expectantly for any answers they may have secured.

"Ma'am," the detective in charge said, "we believe Miss Rucker has given us all she knows and it isn't much. We'll be covering as much ground as quickly as possible in hopes of finding your son and his father without delay. My advice is that you stay home where you can be reached at all times and in the event Kingston decides to drop the child off."

"They do that sometimes," the other detective offered. "They make a rash decision like this out of emotion then reality sets in. You'll need to be home if your boy shows up there."

The two detectives looked as grim and exhausted as Joel felt. But they couldn't possibly have any idea how bad this could get.

Laney thanked the two men and stood like a statue as they moved toward Joel. He braced for whatever bad news they might be about to relay to him that they hadn't wanted to pass on to Laney. He was thankful when she joined Tatum at the bar.

"We have a few calls to make. Outside," the one in charge said. "Ms. Rucker is trying to reach her attorney. We're giving her a few minutes of privacy to do that before we take her in. Make sure she stays put."

The detective's message was loud and clear. Joel had asked for more time with the woman. They were giving it to him. "Count on it."

When they were out the door, he strode to the office.

Margo was fiddling with her cell and swiping at her tears. Joel closed the door and she looked up. "What do you want?" she demanded.

He pulled a chair over to sit knee-to-knee

with her. "The police will be taking you to booking in a few minutes."

She blinked back more tears.

"Accessory to felony kidnapping is a serious charge. You'll do time." He leaned forward. "And if the kid dies, you'll end up on death row." Even suggesting that travesty out loud ripped him apart inside.

"I told them everything I know." Her voice trembled. "He's the kid's father. I didn't know it was kidnapping. He's just trying to get time with his kid."

"Ignorance of the law won't change the charges, Ms. Rucker. You're in deep trouble here but if you help us find him, maybe I can put in a word."

She dragged in a shaky breath. "How can I help you? I don't know anything else! Don't you think I want to get out of this mess? Terry screwed me over on this."

"Think," Joel pressed. "He won't be stupid enough to go home to his father's or to whatever apartment or hotel he uses for sleeping off his drinking binges. But he will go somewhere. Most likely someplace familiar."

Realization dawned on her face. "That mechanic who works on his cars. Makes 'em go faster or something. He hangs out with him a lot. Even slept in his fancy garage a time or two. He got that car he's driving there."

"Who is this mechanic?"

She shook her head. "I've never been to his place and I only met him once but I've heard 'em talk on the phone before." She frowned in concentration. "Studdard or Stuttart. Something like that. He's a big deal around here. Pimps out the motors instead of the bodies. He's kinda famous. He shouldn't be hard for a guy like you to find."

"Anything else?" Joel pushed. "Any friends? Any place at all that he frequents? A restaurant? A department store?"

She laughed. "Terry doesn't have any real friends. Just the ones like the mechanic who make money off him."

"Do you think he'd go back to Houston?" With the Amber Alert he was far more likely to be caught on any main roads and in the larger cities where there was more of a media and police presence. Joel figured he would lay low someplace out of the way until he figured out his next step, which was probably to bring Buddy back just like the detective said. The guy wasn't ambitious enough to have a real plan.

Kingston might be a drunk but he wasn't stupid enough to purposely hurt the kid.

"No way he'd go near his father. They had a big fight this morning. Terry says he's done with his daddy."

Right. His daddy was his money supply. That would be a short-lived position.

Joel took her phone and entered his cell number into her contact list. "You remember anything or you hear anything, you call me first."

Margo nodded. "I'm really going to jail?"

"I'm afraid so."

Her sobs followed him out the door.

Laney waited for him, her expression hopeful, her eyes still filled with terror.

He hugged her and whispered in her ear. "Have Tatum close up. Get your things. We have a lead."

Her breath caught and she trembled in his arms. Then she nodded and rushed to do as he'd asked.

Whatever he had to do to make this right, Joel intended to make it happen. And when he got his hands on Kingston, he was beating the hell out of him. Then Joel would call the cops and give them the lead he was keeping to himself for now…for entirely selfish reasons. Joel wanted to get his hands on Kingston first.

Chapter Seventeen

Studdard Power Engines, Port Arthur, Texas
Friday, May 31st, 6:15 a.m.

Laney felt numb. She thought of all the times Terry had shown up at her house or the saloon too drunk to walk much less drive. He was careless and selfish. He never thought of anyone but himself.

He'd taken Buddy.

She clutched Mr. Bear tighter to her chest. Buddy wouldn't have wanted to go without his bear or without saying goodbye to her. She kept imagining him crying for her.

Laney closed her eyes and prayed again for God to keep her baby safe. The one thing that gave her any relief at all was that she knew Terry wouldn't intentionally hurt Buddy. But the problem with Terry was that he simply was not capable of taking care of himself, much less a child.

"That looks like him."

At the sound of Joel's voice Laney opened her eyes and searched the street. A blue sports car roared into the parking lot. She and Joel had been sitting here for half an hour waiting for the owner, Rudy Studdard, to show up. Her pulse rate started to climb. Was he finally here? The better question was, would he be able to help them?

Simon Ruhl and one of the nice detectives—she couldn't remember his name—had promised to contact her or Joel immediately if they found anything…if there was an accident or a report from a hospital or any word at all about Buddy.

On the half-hour drive from Beaumont to Port Arthur she had seen one of the massive electronic billboards that displayed the face and contact information of any missing child. Seeing Buddy's face on there had been like a bullet to her heart.

Please let my baby be okay. She was terrified by her personal knowledge of Terry's carelessness. He didn't even have a damned car seat for Buddy. Even though Buddy was five, he was still below the weight requirements to use a seat belt only.

He was just a baby.

Despite the police having already checked

the low-rent apartment in Beaumont that Margo had said Terry had leased, she and Joel had checked it out, as well. They'd gone to all the haunts the woman had mentioned Terry frequented. Simon Ruhl's contact in Houston had gotten a firm "haven't seen or heard from him" when they visited old man Kingston in the middle of the night. Simon was also pushing the police to move faster on getting a warrant for Terry's cell-phone carrier.

Each hour that passed tore another hole in Laney's heart.

They had to find him.

A tall, lanky man climbed out of the sports car and strolled to the entrance of his garage, which looked more like a showroom for new automobiles. But there were mechanic's bays in the rear. The lot was full of fancy sports cars, not unlike the one Studdard drove, that were protected by an electrified high fence. Concertina wire was rolled across the top. The car Laney had taken the bat to was there. Had her actions propelled this nightmare?

Focus, Laney. She had to keep a clear head if she was going to be of any use to Buddy. He would be counting on her to find him. This was a good start.

Terry had definitely been here recently.

They had gone to Studdard's home first

and gotten his wife out of bed. She claimed her husband was out of town and wouldn't be back until morning. And when he got back, she further stated, he would go straight to his shop. She gave Joel the husband's cell number but told him not to waste his time, Studdard never answered it anyway unless it was a client's number that he recognized.

And she had been right.

The wife insisted Studdard would be at the shop between six and seven, no exceptions. His work was his life. She gave the impression of not caring one way or the other as long as the bank account stayed healthy.

"Stay in the Jeep," Joel ordered.

Before she could argue, he got out and called the man's name.

For a moment Laney sat there obediently, too emotionally drained to do any differently.

The man turned, his posture reflecting his apprehension as Joel approached him. Laney was thankful he didn't run. Though Studdard was tall, he was thin. He didn't look like the type to fend off a mugger with his own two hands. His hair was dark and he wore glasses and preppy clothes. Probably expensive. Probably never wore the same getup twice. He and Terry had that in common. Along with the expensive car fetish.

They spoke for a minute and Studdard began to shake his head. Laney's heart sank. Where would they go from here? He had to know something. They had learned that the damned car Terry was driving right now came from this man.

Fury driving her, Laney got out of the Jeep and marched up to the door. Both men looked at her in surprise.

"Mr. Studdard?"

"Laney," Joel said gently. "You should wait in the car."

Studdard looked from her to Joel and back. "I haven't seen Kingston since the day before yesterday when he dropped his damaged car off here and borrowed a loaner."

"But you've talked before," Laney accused, desperate. "Maybe gone out for a meal together. Surely he's mentioned places he likes to hang out or places he might have been or be planning to go." She needed something from this man!

Studdard sighed. "Why don't you come inside and I'll see what I can do." He shrugged. "I know a few others he's done *business* with." He looked at Joel. "If you know what I mean."

"Are you referring to drugs, Mr. Studdard?" she asked.

Laney steeled for worse news. If Terry had

gotten into drugs… Oh, God. Her body started to quake. As strong as she wanted to be for Buddy, she couldn't keep the fear at bay.

"Yes. Very recently. That's why I limit my dealings with him to strictly business. I won't take the risk. My clients are the rich and powerful. Whatever they do behind closed doors, they have no desire to do business with anyone with a less-than-stellar reputation."

Laney thought of all the horror stories she had seen on the news where people sold their children for money to buy drugs. Bile burned her throat. But Terry had money… Or had his father really cut him off completely?

Inside, Studdard locked the front entrance behind them and flipped on the lights. "No one else will be here before eight-thirty. I like coming in early to get paperwork done."

"We appreciate your help, Studdard," Joel said. "A missing child requires the attention of everyone who knows the person responsible."

Studdard pushed his glasses up his nose. "Certainly."

He led the way through the showroom of expensive-looking cars. In his office, he flipped on the lights and gestured to the chairs in front of his desk.

"I never gave Terry my personal numbers." He glanced at Laney. "I only do that with close,

trustworthy associates. He has this number."
He indicated the phone on his desk. "If he
called me, the number will be on the caller ID
and if he wanted something he will have left
a voice mail."

Laney prayed he was right. She sat on the
edge of her seat. Joel stood behind her.

"Several calls," Studdard muttered as he
scrolled through the numbers. He paused, studied the screen on his desk phone. "And there
he is. He called at two thirty-eight this morning." He hit the button to play his voice mails.

Laney held her breath.

He skipped through four calls before Terry's
voice floated from the machine. "Studdard, I
have a situation."

Thank God he didn't sound wasted. Hope
dared to swell in her chest.

"I need another car. ASAP. I can't come to
your shop so bring it to the coffeehouse on 365.
I'll be waiting. I've got cash. If anyone comes
looking for me, you didn't get this call. Screw
me over and I'll tell your wife about your ex-
tracurricular activities. Hey, and bring me one
of your car seats."

Laney gasped, the sound ragged.

Red climbed Studdard's face. "I hope—"
He cleared his throat "I hope...this helps in
some way."

"Let's go," Joel said. "You're going to help a lot more."

Studdard reared back in his chair. "I've already—"

"He knows my Jeep," Joel argued. "He's expecting you and a new ride. That's what he's going to get." Studdard started to argue again but Joel shut him up with a raised hand. "If this guy gets spooked he could run. A high-speed chase could have a bad ending."

Studdard blinked twice.

"You help us," Joel offered, "and the police don't have to be involved. No one has to know you help friends out this way. Clearly Kingston felt comfortable relaying he had a situation. And considering he's not one of your *trustworthy* clients, I can only guess what you will and have done for those folks."

Laney was holding her breath again, tears brimming on her lashes. She should have gone to the house for her gun. Then, by God, this guy wouldn't hesitate. Joel had a handgun in his Jeep. He had showed it to her. But Joel insisted he never used it unless there was no other recourse.

Studdard finally acquiesced. "All right."

He selected a modified, as he called it, two-door he felt confident Terry would like. Laney rode in the front with him since she was small enough to hunker down in the floorboard when they approached Terry's car. Joel was slouched down across the tiny backseat since there was no way he could get enough of his big body below the level of the dashboard up front.

Laney consoled herself with memories of her baby. From the first time he had smiled up at her at two months old, she had known they were going to be fine. They had each other and the rest would fall into place in time.

She had let him down.

The drive took less than ten minutes but each one felt like a lifetime to Laney. Daylight had chased away the darkness but the rising sun did nothing to rid her of the chill that had settled deep in her bones.

Her baby had been missing for over eight hours now. Her soul cried out in anguish.

There was a fair-size crowd at the coffee-house but Terry's car wasn't in the lot. He'd parked across the street in the parking lot of a defunct gas station. He had backed up to the building, so that his vehicle pointed toward the street.

For a fast getaway, Laney supposed. Or maybe to hide his license plate in case the police were looking for him.

"Nose up to him," Joel told Studdard. "We don't want him trying to take off."

Laney hunkered down in the seat. Studdard did as Joel ordered.

"Shut off the engine and get out," Joel told him.

"Okay." The man's voice shook a little now. His fingers fumbled on the keys.

"Stay calm, Studdard," Joel urged. "We have reason to believe he's armed."

"What?" Studdard turned around in his seat. "You didn't say anything about that before."

"Get out of the car," Joel growled. "He's not going to shoot you. He thinks you're here to help. You want him thinking you're not?"

Studdard adjusted his glasses. "But he's just sitting there. Why doesn't he get out?"

Enough of the debating and second-guessing. Laney grabbed the door handle and wrenched the door open. To hell with Studdard. She bailed out with Joel trying his best to grab her and drag her back into the car.

She stormed up to the driver's side of Terry's car. "I want my boy, you son of—"

Laney's knees buckled. Joel caught her before she hit the ground.

There was a hole in Terry's chest… Blood had soaked his shirt and…run down onto the seat between his legs. Where was Buddy? She couldn't see him…not in the front seat or the back.

A surge of adrenaline hit Laney. She jerked

from Joel's hold and reached for the door. "I have to find Buddy!"

Joel grabbed her back. "Don't touch anything, Laney."

"I have to find my baby." How had this happened? Who had taken her baby if he wasn't with his father? Was he cowering in the back floorboard? "Buddy! It's mommy! Where are you, baby?"

Joel gave her a gentle shake. "Let me look, okay? This is a crime scene now and we have to be careful. If whoever did this took Buddy, we can't risk contaminating evidence."

Blackness threatened. Laney barely hung on. Terry was dead. Buddy was gone. Whoever had taken Buddy was willing to kill….

Joel braced her against the wall away from Terry's car. Her body felt cold and hot at once. She couldn't draw a deep enough breath. Where was her baby? What had Terry done? Who had done this to him? Was there even enough room in the rear floorboard for Buddy to hide? Why wouldn't he have cried out to her when he heard her voice?

Because he wasn't here…. Her heart lurched.

Joel moved around to the other side of the car and opened the passenger side door. Laney dared to move away from the wall. Her legs felt rubbery but she managed to stay vertical.

Joel fumbled in the glove box then withdrew from the passenger side as the trunk popped open.

Laney's heart hit the concrete. She hadn't thought of that. Her knees went weak again. *No. Please don't let him be in there....*

After a quick survey of the truck's interior, Joel closed the lid and shook his head.

A crazy mixture of relief and renewed fear flooded her veins. What did this mean? Who would take her little boy?

A drug dealer? A person who wanted to sell her baby to human traffickers or some sick pedophile?

Her heart rose and started to thunder. How would they ever be able to find Buddy now?

Joel's words drifted to her through the haze of panic. He was on the phone. He stated the address and then said that he wanted to report a homicide. He'd called the police.

Dear God. Why would anyone do this? What kind of people had Terry gotten himself involved with?

Images filled her head. Stick figures all lined up in a row...dozens and dozens of them on that motel wall.

She'd watched Buddy through his bedroom window.

The grandma lady...the murderer.

Port Arthur Police Station, 8:30 a.m.

JOEL HAD BEEN INTERROGATED BEFORE. The Port
Arthur detective along with the two from
Beaumont had questioned him repeatedly
about the incident in the High Noon parking
lot when Kingston and Joel had exchanged
heated words.

Anger came and went as Joel wrestled with
his emotions. These guys had a job to do and
Joel understood that. But there was a child
missing and these guys should be helping look
for him, not rehashing irrelevant information.

They'd run Joel's prints just to be sure he
was who he said he was. Simon Ruhl had
called and offered to come to the station but
Joel knew he needed to be on the search for
Lucas. The sooner Lucas was found, the sooner
Simon and the others could help with this situation.

God almighty, the situation had gone to hell
fast.

He'd come here to protect Laney and Buddy
and he'd failed.

A female detective was questioning Laney.
He wished she didn't have to go through this.
Until they released them there wasn't a whole
hell of a lot Joel could do.

"Well, all right," the detective from Beaumont in charge of Buddy's case finally announced. "We're going to request support from the FBI. For now, I believe it would be in the best interest of all if you took Ms. Seagers home. We're doing everything that can be done at this time."

Joel stood. "I can appreciate that, but you need to appreciate what she's going through. Sitting around waiting isn't the answer for her peace of mind."

The detective nodded. "We do understand. We'll contact you if we learn anything new."

Joel turned for the door but the detective spoke again. "And for the love of Mike, call us if you get a lead and let us follow up. There's a far less likelihood of the evidence being contaminated."

Joel tossed back the man's own words. "We understand."

Joel walked out. He wasn't making any promises he wouldn't keep. He followed the corridor back to the lobby area. Laney sat in a chair looking devastated and lost. She didn't even look up as he approached.

He sat down beside her. She blinked but didn't look at him.

From the moment he confirmed that

Kingston was dead, Joel knew with complete certainty that his murder and Buddy's disappearance had nothing to do with drugs or human trafficking or some sick pedophile.

Clare Barker and Weeden had been watching. Kingston's desperate move had provided an opportunity. Clare had been taken with Buddy—that was obvious. She wanted him. Maybe to reel in Laney.

All Joel had to do was find those two and he would find Buddy. He felt certain of that. For now the boy was likely safe. If the goal was to lure in Laney, they would need Buddy alive.

With the Amber Alert, Lucas missing and Terry's murder, Clare Barker was now wanted for questioning by the police as well as the Colby Agency. She couldn't afford to be out in the open. She and Weeden would need to find someplace to lay low where no one would look for them. Someplace one or both considered safe and way off the radar.

"If you were Clare Barker," Joel said quietly, "where would you go to hide with the grandson you had been dying to spend time with?"

Laney looked over at him. "You think she took him?"

Her voice wobbled. Joel nodded.

"She must've taken him. We have to find

her, Joel. We have to. I read those articles that were in the photo album," she said. "Their farm was off the beaten path. No one lives there."

Joel managed a weak smile. That was his thinking, too.

Some of the victims' families had bought the place in a tax auction years ago. They'd boarded it up and swore that no one would ever live there again.

"No one would look there," Joel offered. "It's too obvious." He tugged at a strand of her hair. "You know, like in the movies, when you just know the bad guy can't be a certain cliché character because it would be too much of a no-brainer."

Her lips trembled into a faint smile of her own and she nodded.

"I say we take off and head there right now. We could be in Granger by one, maybe sooner since we've missed most of the morning commuters."

"There's nothing else we can do here." Anticipation tinged her voice.

He shook his head. "Nothing. Except wait."

Laney pushed to her feet. "I don't want to wait."

Joel stood. He took her hand in his. "We will find him." She turned to him, her usually glittering brown eyes clouded with fear and misery. "That's a promise," he guaranteed.

As they exited the police station Joel prayed he would be able to keep that promise.

Chapter Eighteen

Clare had rocked the boy to sleep. It had taken a while. He'd slept most of the way here but when he'd awakened he had cried for his mother.

She had used this old rocker to sway her girls to sleep when they were little. She was glad it was still here. Much of the old furniture was still here. The house had fallen into grave disrepair, but that could all be fixed in time. She and her family could make something of the place. Turn it back into a real home.

"Sweet boy." She gently brushed the hair out of his face. He was an angel. Beautiful and perfect in every way. Just like his mother was. She had been almost this age when Clare last held her. She had been crying for her bear just as Buddy had cried for his.

Clare wasn't sure how Tony had managed to

get the boy away from that rotten father of his
but she was glad he had. She hadn't asked any
questions and, as usual, her son had offered
no explanations. To Clare's way of thinking,
Tony was a hero for rescuing Buddy. No man
like that drunkard Terry Kingston deserved to
have this precious angel.

Now Lisa would want to come to Clare.
Tony's plan was a good one. She had worried
about how she would convince her daughters to
come to her. Especially with the Colby Agency
working against her.

The floor creaked and Clare looked up. Tony
hovered in the doorway. He looked away when
her gaze met his.

"He's precious, isn't he?"

Tony nodded.

She had never gotten to hold him this way.
Clare wondered if Janet or the Weedens, the
people who had ultimately adopted Tony, had
ever once been kind to him. The thought of
what they may have done to him besides what
was obvious made her sick to her stomach.
Clare hadn't known the Weedens but Janet had.
Since her release, Clare had learned that the
Weedens had been a bad bunch. They were all
gone now. The old man and woman had died
years ago. Not soon enough for Clare's lik-
ing. They had been immensely cruel to Tony

if half of what she had learned about them was true. No matter what Tony said about the accident that had caused the loss of his arm, Clare feared the injury had been the result of something far more sinister. She knew her sister too well. Janet had benefited financially from the adoptions of Clare's girls and she suspected the loathsome witch had done the same when she turned Tony over to the Weedens.

"Lunch is ready," Tony announced. "Ham and cheese sandwiches with all the fixings."

Clare caressed the child's soft cheek. "I'll be there in a minute."

"I cut the tomatoes fresh," he snapped. "If you wait, the bread will be soggy."

Clare looked up at him and wondered if watching her with Buddy made him envious. She wished she could change that. Take away the hurt from the past.

But what was done was done and she had made many mistakes. The most she could hope for was forgiveness or perhaps not even that. If they could all just start over from here, that would be enough.

She looked around at the room that had once been her girls' bedroom. The place was old and run-down for sure. The yard looked like a mess. The clinic that had once been a barn was falling in.

At least the dead who had been buried here had been moved. That was something. The past was behind her now and she wanted to forget those ugly years.

Tony shuffled away. The sound drew her attention to the door. She had disappointed him enough. The least she could do was eat the meal he had prepared.

Anything to make him happy. He had done so very much for her and was prepared to do more.

She placed Buddy carefully on the throw she'd spread on the floor. There was no pillow or proper covers but it would do for now. Children his age could sleep through a war.

Truth was, they were caught up in a war. The battle had scarcely begun.

Tony had told her this morning about his savings. He had plenty of money, he'd said, to fix the old place up if he could buy it back.

That would be nice.

When she had accomplished her goal the world would know the truth and perhaps her home would be returned to her. Wouldn't it be nice if Rafe lived to hear of her good fortune? He would tear out his hair. She prayed he would suffer every minute of every hour until they shoved those needles into his loathsome veins.

Clare left the room and went in search of her dear son. She owed him so much.

She had seen the spots of blood on his shirt when he brought Buddy to her. But that was irrelevant in this war they were waging. Whatever he had done to bring her grandson to her, she needed to properly show her appreciation.

It was the least she could do with him so willing to sacrifice so much for her.

Tony waited in the kitchen. He had stocked a cooler with fresh sandwich meats and drinks. He thought of everything. Clare wasn't sure what she would have done without him. He seemed prepared for every situation. He had flashlights and changes of clothes. Maps and money. He said that they would find new transportation soon. His idea to come here, the last place anyone would look, was genius.

He was her hero.

A good son.

Clare smiled as she picked up the sandwich he had made. "This is so much better than anything I was ever served in that awful place."

He ducked his head in acknowledgment of her praise. Her son didn't say much but he provided more than she deserved. He had overcome much in his life. Like her, he was a survivor.

They ate in silence for a few moments. Clare

didn't like the silence. She had endured far too much of it in prison. She'd had no one to talk to. No one who cared if she lived or died. "Did you find a place to hide the car?"

"Down the road in the turnoff that leads into the woods to an old burned-out house."

"Where the old Martin house once stood." She remembered when the house burned. She and Rafe had just moved here in what the weathermen had called the worst winter in Texas history. Like their old house, the Martins' had nothing but a fireplace to keep warm. It was a terrible tragedy. The whole family was lost in the fire.

Tony shrugged. "Guess so. It's easy to find through the woods beyond the barn."

Barn... He meant the clinic. Where she and Rafe had done their work...when they were happy so, so long ago.

"We can get there quickly if need be," her son noted.

He was worried that they would be found here. But with their photos all over the news now, their options were limited. In truth, taking Buddy hadn't likely been a good idea but she would not spoil her son's glory. His intentions had been good. And she had so desperately wanted to get to know her grandson.

More silence followed. Clare hoped Tony

wasn't regretting having helped her. He seemed to have less and less to say to her with each passing day, even if he accomplished more.

The sound of crying broke the silence. Buddy had awakened. Poor child, he was probably terrified.

"I'll get him," Tony grumbled.

"You finish your lunch." Clare set her sandwich aside and started across the room. "I'll get him."

Tony turned sharply. "Wait."

The feral look on his face scared her. Her fingers balled into fists to contain her fear. "What's wrong?"

He rushed past her. She followed, her movements stiff with uncertainty. He moved to the front window in the entry hall next to the door and peeked out the grimy glass.

Her heart started to pound with the fear swooshing through her veins. "Is something wrong?"

Tony wheeled around. "Go to the car now. I'll get the boy."

Fear snaked around her heart. "The police?"

"Go!" he commanded. "I'll bring the boy."

Clare rushed out the back door and across the yard, the blood pounding in her ears. She fled deep into the woods before she dared to stop.

She gasped for air and tried to hear above

the sound of her own heartbeat. How many were here? Her journey could not end this way. There was still much to do. She hadn't found Olivia yet. She wanted to—

A scream filled the air.

Her heart stopped.

Buddy.

Chapter Nineteen

Beaumont Hospital, 1:15 p.m.

Victoria waited in the lobby, her body numb with fear. The relief she had felt at finding Lucas had been short-lived once the E.R. physicians had examined him.

His right shoulder had been dislocated and his left leg was fractured. But the worst was the head injury. A serious concussion. Once the CT scan was completed they would know the extent of the damage.

Victoria closed her eyes. For nearly twenty-four hours they had searched for him. The last six very near the area where he had been found by a passing motorist.

The thick canopy of trees had hidden his rented sedan from view as the helicopter they'd hired had made pass after pass over the area. Lucas had suffered hours of agony because Victoria could not find him.

Clare Barker and Weeden were responsible for this. Fury unleashed inside Victoria. Lucas had told his rescuers how Weeden had forced him to take the ditch to prevent a horrendous collision that might have killed them all.

He had lain unconscious for hours. When he'd awakened he had endured the pain of scrambling into the passenger floorboard for his cell. But there had been no service. He'd had no choice but to start the slow, agonizing effort of trying to pull his damaged body up that embankment to the road.

Victoria prayed Lucas had suffered no permanent damage.

She opened her eyes and took stock of the deserted lobby. Even the reception desk had a bell one could ring if service was required. Victoria was alone. Simon and Jim had been here with her until half an hour ago. She had dismissed them. There was nothing either of them could do. They were needed in the search for Buddy Seagers. Victoria would take care of her husband.

Please let him be okay.

All those months ago they had made the decision that they would retire, and look at them now. Lucas was chasing the bad guys as if he were closer to thirty than sixty. And she was no better. Ferreting out the secrets of heinous killers.

What had she been thinking?

She would see that this never happened again. Never. She and her husband were going to make that lifestyle change they had promised to make. Jim was handling the agency in Chicago beautifully and Simon had the Houston office well on its way to fully staffed.

There was no need for her and her husband to be involved in the day-to-day operations. A nice cottage on the beach and long walks in the sand were far more suitable for the years that lay ahead of them.

Victoria would attend to that just as soon as she ensured the woman and her accomplice who had done this to Lucas were captured and paid sufficiently for their crimes. And if Rafe Barker was innocent, which she sincerely doubted, she would set the record straight on that, as well.

"Mrs. Camp?"

Victoria rose, her heart thundering madly as she met the doctor's gaze. "Yes?"

"You may see your husband now."

Thank God.

As Victoria moved toward the door that separated the lobby from the E.R., the doctor explained, "Mr. Camp does have a concussion so we're going to keep him here for a couple of days given his other injuries." The doctor smiled. "But he's going to be fine. In fact, I may need your help in convincing him to stay put. He's rather stubborn."

The good doctor didn't know the half of it. Victoria gave him a reassuring smile. "He'll stay as long as you feel is necessary, Doctor."

He paused at a door in the long corridor. "I'll give the two of you some privacy."

Victoria thanked him and entered the room. She suspected the doctor wanted no part in the debate that would follow. No worries. There would be no debate. She had made her decision and Lucas was not going to sway her.

Her heart melted and her lips spread into a smile when she caught sight of her husband on the examining table, a print cotton gown his only attire. His forehead was bandaged, covering the nasty gash. His right arm was in a sling and his left leg sported a walking cast. But he looked like heaven on earth to Victoria. He was alive, with no injury from which he couldn't recover.

"I suppose it could be worse," she announced as she crossed to his bedside.

He smiled through the pain. She wondered if they had given him any pain medication. The nurse had said it was necessary to wait until after the CT scan for any pain meds.

"I told you I'd be fine."

Victoria had cried copious tears when they'd found him. She wouldn't cry now. She was far too irritated, mostly at herself, and she intended to reveal no weakness. "You knew better than to follow a mark without backup or at least informing someone of your whereabouts. You've done this work far too long to be so careless."

"Correct on all counts, my dear."

The irritation gave way to those softer emotions she had attempted to conceal. "You scared me to death, Lucas."

He took her hand in his and held it tenderly. "I am more sorry about that than you can know." He winked to hide the emotion shining in his own eyes, but she saw it. "Quite frankly, I scared myself."

"Never again." She shook her head firmly.

He started to nod then winced. "Whatever you say, darling."

Victoria couldn't restrain herself any longer. She leaned down and kissed him squarely on the mouth. He caressed her cheek and smiled beneath her onslaught.

"I love you, Victoria."

She blinked back those confounding tears. "I was so afraid I'd lost you."

He squeezed her hand. "You gave me the strength to climb out of that ravine. I knew you would be worried. I wasn't about to let you down."

She managed a wobbling smile. "Very well. I suppose all is forgiven, under the circumstances."

"Good. Let's get out of here. We need to help Laney and Hayden find Buddy."

"All our resources are focused on the search." She tucked the sheet around him. "You and I are staying here for a day or two."

When he started to argue, she reminded him, "'Whatever you say, darling.'"

Lucas surrendered.

She had known he would.

Lucas Camp was a man of his word.

Chapter Twenty

Laney froze.

The scream echoed over and over in her head.

"Buddy." His name whispered from her lips.

"Call the police and then Simon," Joel called back at her as he rushed toward the house. "He's not that far behind us."

But they were all too late. Her son was screaming. The screams from her dreams echoed in her brain. Swelled and twisted with the sound of her son's scream.

Laney stared at the house.

This was the place…the screaming place… where the darkness waited. The place of nightmares and the smell of blood and terror.

Laney couldn't breathe. Tears crowded her eyes, her throat.

"Mommy!"

"Buddy," she murmured.

He was here…. And he needed her.

Laney snapped into action. She ran toward the sound of Buddy's scream, her trembling fingers fumbling with the phone.

A gunshot blasted the air. She jerked to a halt. "Buddy! Where are you, baby?"

Nothing. She started running again. She cleared the back of the house, stalled in the yard and turned all the way around. Where was he? Where was Joel? "Mommy's here! Buddy!"

The police! Call the police! Laney hit the necessary buttons.

The dispatcher's voice sounded scratchy, as if the reception was bad. "Nine-one-one, what is the nature of your emergency?"

"Someone took my son." Laney's body shook. Her throat tried to close. "I heard him scream! Gunshots. I need help!"

Another gun blast pierced the air.

"Please! Help us!" she cried.

"Give me your address, ma'am."

The address! What was the address? Laney shook herself, took a breath, then gave the address.

"Stay on the line, ma'am, we—"

Laney couldn't wait. She shoved the phone into her pocket and rushed into the woods calling her son's name.

JOEL CUT THROUGH THE TREES. Another shot whizzed past his head. He ducked.

Up ahead, a male figure with dark hair and wearing a white T-shirt zigzagged through the trees. Weeden.

Joel couldn't get a clear visual on Weeden. Was he carrying Buddy?

Joel lunged forward, keeping low. He cut through the brush and trees making way too much noise. There was no help for it; he couldn't slow down.

If he could get a clear shot…

He stalled.

Nothing moved.

No sound.

Joel forced his heart rate to slow. He listened beyond the sound of his own pounding heart.

"Buddy!"

Laney.

A blast echoed in the air.

Was the son of a bitch shooting at her?

Joel rushed from his hiding place, making all the noise he could, to draw Weeden's attention.

A blast thundered and a bullet hit the tree to his right.

Joel hit the ground. As he lay there, he listened.

Where was that bastard?

Where was Laney?

"Buddy! It's Mommy!"

The voice came from his left.

Joel scrambled up and moved forward and to the right, once again making all the noise he could.

Another shot…hit the ground beside him. Way too close.

Weeden was close.

A flurry of movement drew Joel's attention to his right. He eased between the trees, careful of every step.

He caught a glimpse of dark hair.

Weeden.

Joel moved closer.

"Mommy!"

Buddy.

Joel turned just as the blast echoed. He jerked with the impact, felt the burn of the bullet low on his left side…

He pivoted, used the nearest tree for cover. He touched his side with his free hand. Warm blood oozed between his fingers. *Damn it.*

He had to protect Buddy and Laney. He couldn't let this guy get close to them.

Adrenaline fired through him, and he ignored the pain and rushed forward. Something white flashed between the trees to his left. The

T-shirt. The bastard was headed toward the sound of Laney's voice…. Toward Buddy.

Joel charged in that direction.

He spotted Weeden, running…ten yards ahead.

Joel aimed. The bastard darted left. Joel couldn't get the shot without firing into the brush. But Buddy could be in there.

He moved in a dead run parallel with Weeden's path, but suddenly Weeden turned and Joel ducked for cover.

A shot echoed. Bark flew off the tree just above his head. Weeden was shooting to kill.

Fury lashed through Joel. He couldn't throw out any cover shots without looking first. Laney or Buddy could be out there anywhere.

Joel eased from behind the tree, scanned the area around him and moved forward.

"Buddy!" Laney cried.

Joel turned toward the sound of her voice. She was too close.

Another gun blast echoed.

Hot metal tore through his left shoulder and Joel snapped back with the impact.

Weeden darted through the trees.

Fighting through the burn, Joel leveled a bead on him and fired.

Weeden went down.

Relief rushed through Joel, helping him to ignore the pain.

His left arm hanging limply at his side, Joel ran toward the position where Weeden had fallen.

He stopped, studied the ground.

There was blood…but no Weeden.

Joel took stock of the woods around him as he followed the blood trail. The bastard couldn't have gotten far.

A wave of weakness washed over Joel.

He grunted with the pain of lifting his left hand high enough to press his palm over the hole in his side. Sweat poured down his face.

He listened for movement. No sound. No screams… No Laney calling for her son.

He couldn't risk calling out to her or to Buddy.

The ground moved under his feet.

Hold it together.

He had to find this crazy SOB.

Wood snapped behind him.

Joel froze, swayed, then steadied himself to turn—

Something solid slammed into the back of his skull.

He went down.

The sky and trees spun wildly.

Weeden stared down at him, the barrel of his weapon aimed at Joel's face.

"Stop!"

The scream sucked Joel into the darkness.

"BUDDY!" LANEY RUSHED through the woods. She stumbled. She had to find her baby!

Where was Joel?

The gunshots had stopped.... But where was her baby?

She called his name again.

Dear God, please let me find my baby!

Run! Find him! She stumbled again, caught herself and kept going.

"Buddy!"

Where were the monsters who had her baby?

"Joel?"

She cleared the tree line and found herself staring at the back of the old house. A rusty creaking noise floated across the air as the wind shifted one of the old swings.

Wait... She should be going the other way—into the woods. She wasn't supposed to come back to the house. Was she? She hadn't heard Buddy's voice anymore. Where was he?

In the woods. She had to go back in there.

Her baby was in the woods with those awful people. She'd heard someone scream "stop." Not Buddy or Joel.

She turned back to the woods and cried out her son's name. They were in there somewhere.

Why didn't Buddy or Joel answer her?

"Mommy!"

Buddy burst from the woods.

A sound escaped Laney's throat as she hurried to meet him.

She scooped him up and hugged him close, tears blurring her vision. He sobbed against her shoulder, his little body trembling.

"It's okay, baby. Mommy's got you now."

Her breath was trapped in her lungs. Those people were still out there. She had to get Buddy to safety. She needed to find Joel.

Laney's gaze cleared. She turned to run and something in the trees—right where Buddy had come from the woods—caught her attention.

The woman... Gray hair cropped to her chin. A pink dress.

She stared at Laney. Laney stared back. She couldn't move.

Was she coming after Buddy again? Laney told herself to run, but she felt paralyzed.

They just kept staring at each other.

Laney had no idea how many seconds passed but the woman suddenly turned away and disappeared into the woods.

Clare Barker...*her mother*.

More seconds elapsed before Laney could move.

Where was Joel?

Was Weeden still out there? There had been no more gunshots, but could she risk Buddy's safety by running into the woods to look for Joel?

She had to do something. Buddy started to shift around in her arms but his sobbing had eased.

Joel could be injured. She had to find him.

With a big breath, Laney held on tight to her son and rushed back into the woods. "Joel!"

The wail of sirens stalled her. Thank God. She turned and ran as fast as she could toward the front yard.

The third police car skidded to a halt in front of the house as she rounded the corner. Her knees went weak with relief but she kept going.

"We have to find Joel," she shouted to the first officer out of his car. "He's out there...."

"Calm down, ma'am, and tell us what happened."

Laney's mind abruptly cleared. There was no time to waste. "A man and woman kidnapped my son. We found them here. The man is armed. My...friend rushed into the woods after him. There were gunshots. He may be hurt." She broke down then. "You have to find him."

Buddy started to wail. She tried to comfort him but her tears only made him cry harder.

The other officers had already fanned out across the yard but they weren't moving fast enough.

"They have to hurry," she urged. "He could be hurt. The other man had a gun. There were a lot of gunshots." Joel should have come out of the woods by now. He was hurt. Laney knew it. She just knew it. "You have to do something!" she shouted at the officer.

"Ma'am," the officer said calmly, "are you or the child injured?"

She shook her head. What was he waiting for? He needed to find Joel.

"You and your son get in the car where you'll be safe and we'll find your friend."

He didn't get it. "Joel is out there and he needs help. He would be back here by now if not." She was repeating herself but no one was listening. The renewed burn of tears glazed her eyes.

A dark SUV roared to a stop on the road.

Three men emerged. The officer rested his hand on his weapon as if unsure of what would happen next.

"Laney, are you and Buddy all right?"

It was Simon Ruhl.

She rushed to him. "Joel is still out there. There were a lot of gunshots." Her knees went weak again.

Simon turned to one of the other men. "Take care of Ms. Seagers and her son." To the other, he said, "Let's go."

Feeling helpless, Laney watched as Simon and the other man, along with the officer who'd been trying to calm her, rushed across the yard.

Please, please, let Joel be okay.

Buddy drew back to look at her. His face was drawn in a frown and his eyes were red from crying. "That bad man tried to take me away."

"Did he hurt you, baby?" A new fear trembled through Laney. She prayed they hadn't hurt him in any way. Dear God, she had only just thought of that. What kind of monsters were these people?

Buddy shook his head resolutely. "They didn't hurt me. But I wanted to go home so I got away."

She managed a shaky smile. "What a strong boy you are. You found your way back to Mommy."

This time when he shook his head, his eyes were big. "No, no, Mommy. I couldn't find you. I was lost in the trees. The grandma lady brought me to you."

Laney stilled. She moistened her lips. The memory of the woman staring at her from the edge of the woods flashed in Laney's brain. "Are you sure, baby? Weren't she and the bad man trying to take you away from Mommy?"

"Nope. It was the bad man with the stubby thing." He patted his upper arm. "He took me from Terry. When I woke up I was with the grandma lady."

So Weeden kidnapped Buddy and took him to Clare. He had killed Terry to get to Buddy. The impact of that realization abruptly penetrated the layers of fear that had been swaddling her brain. Terry was dead. No matter how miserable he had made Laney he hadn't deserved to be murdered. Agony swelled in her chest.

"The grandma lady helped me find you." Buddy laid his head on Laney's shoulder. "She's nice."

Laney hugged him so tight he squirmed. Thank God he was safe. Her baby just didn't understand that the woman was not nice. He had no idea.

The man from the Colby Agency standing beside Laney was saying something. She turned to him but he was on his cell phone. She didn't even know his name.

Why hadn't they found Joel yet?

She opened her mouth to demand that this man watch Buddy while she went to search for Joel. After all, there was no need for both of them to be standing here. But he spoke first.

"They've found Hayden. EMS will be here any second. They were notified as soon as the Granger police were on the scene."

What did that mean? "How badly is he hurt?"

"I'm sorry, ma'am, I can't answer that."

Laney tilted Buddy's chin up. "Mommy needs to go help Mr. Joel so I need you to stay with this gentleman until I get back."

"Ma'am, it would be best for you to stay here."

Buddy clung to her. She couldn't leave him like that and she couldn't risk taking him back into those woods. There was no way to know where Clare and Weeden were at this point. Laney's heart twisted in agony, She prayed Joel wasn't hurt too badly.

Just when she thought her heart would be crushed with worry, four men, two of them uniformed officers, rounded the corner of the house carrying Joel between them.

Laney rushed to meet them, her heart thundering. "How is he?"

"He's unconscious," Simon answered. "We can't assess the full extent of his injuries but he's breathing and his pulse is strong."

As they reached the front yard, the ambulance arrived.

Laney stayed back while the paramedics did their work. Joel's face was ashen. His shirt was bloody around one shoulder and along his side. He didn't move. Didn't open his eyes. She struggled not to cry. She didn't want to upset Buddy any further but she was scared to death. There was so much blood.

Finally, they loaded Joel onto a gurney and headed for the ambulance.

She hurried along beside them. "Is he going to be okay?"

"We hope so," one of the paramedics said without looking at her.

Fear lanced her heart. Why couldn't anyone tell her what she wanted to hear?

"Laney."

She turned to Simon, who gestured to his SUV. "Come with us. We're following the ambulance."

He helped her and Buddy into the SUV. Laney couldn't take her eyes off the ambulance.

The ambulance spun away. Simon maneuvered the SUV onto the road behind it. The police stayed at the farm to look for Weeden and Clare Barker.

But they were gone.

Simon introduced her to the other two men. The only name that stuck was Colby. One was named Jim Colby. She remembered Lucas mentioning him.... He was Victoria's son.

The men spoke quietly but Laney wasn't really listening. She kept thinking about the way the woman, Clare, had looked at her. What did she want? Was she giving the orders? Had she told Weeden to kill whoever got in their way?

Laney closed her eyes. She had Buddy back safe and sound. If Joel was okay, those two things were all that mattered at the moment.

Clare Barker could disappear and never come back for all Laney cared. She wished she had never heard that name.

Chapter Twenty-One

Beaumont Hospital, 6:05 p.m.

Laney paced the small E.R. waiting room. Buddy was asleep in a chair. Bless his heart. When he woke up he would be wild with a sudden burst of energy. She wished she could take a power nap right now and wake up refreshed.

But that was impossible. She didn't dare close her eyes.

She'd taken Buddy to the hospital cafeteria and he'd eaten like he was totally starved. But he had assured her that the grandma lady had fed him.

Simon had called and briefed her on what they and the police had found. Weeden had taken at least one bullet. They had followed the blood trail to an old, burned-out house down the road from the former Barker residence. And that was where the trail ended. It was believed that Clare and Weeden had left their getaway car there.

The police had an APB out for both Clare and Weeden along with the description of their car. Hospitals and clinics had been alerted to be on the watch for a wounded one-armed man.

Simon felt certain they would not seek medical assistance unless the injury was life-threatening. Weeden was a nurse so as long as he was conscious he could instruct his mother in how to attend to his wound.

Laney stopped midway across the lobby. She kept thinking about how the woman had stared at her. About the house and how it had felt to be there. The screams from her lifelong nightmares had come from that house. Laney knew that now.

Whatever had happened in that house, as a four-year-old child she had blocked the memories. She wondered if the older one, Olivia, remembered anything more clearly.

Laney stared beyond the glass wall that separated the E.R. waiting room from the emergency parking area outside. News crews had gathered.

The world now knew that Clare Barker had left prison with an agenda to find her daughters who were, in fact, alive.

Laney had two sisters.

"Laney."

She turned at the sound of her name, her heart rushing into her throat. But it was not a nurse or a doctor. The woman's dark hair was sprinkled with gray but rather than looking old, she looked sophisticated. Her face was very attractive and she wore an elegant suit. Was she someone from the hospital staff? Was she about to deliver news that Laney did not want to hear?

"Yes?" Laney held her breath.

"My name is Victoria Colby-Camp. Do you have any news on Joel's condition?"

Laney was so exhausted she wasn't sure whether to be relieved or disappointed. "Nothing yet. He's been in surgery for two hours. But he was stable and had regained consciousness before they took him to surgery." Laney was still furious they hadn't let her see him.

But, if they made him well again, she could live with that.

Victoria smiled. "Joel is strong and determined. Like my Lucas."

"Oh, gosh. Your husband is here. How is he?" Joel had gotten the call en route to Granger that Lucas had been found. That was how Simon and his entourage were able to arrive so quickly after her and Joel. Joel had explained their suspicions to Simon. And since Lucas had been located, Simon and his team headed that way, as well.

"He's fine," Victoria said. "We expect to be able to go home in a day or two."

"That's great." Laney had so much she wanted to say to this woman but she was absolutely drained and nothing in her head was straight. "I want to thank you for all your agency has done to protect my boy and me."

Victoria peeked past her and smiled. "Your son is an amazing young man. Simon told me how well he handled this ordeal."

Pride welled in Laney's chest. "He is something." She just hoped she could get over the idea of never letting him out of her sight again. Laney turned back to Victoria. "Things might have turned out way different if it hadn't been for you and your agency." She shook her head. "I don't know what we would have done without Joel."

Victoria took Laney's hand in hers and gave it a squeeze. "We will continue to ensure your safety until this is done. You have my word."

A fresh wave of tears filled Laney's eyes. "Thank you." With Buddy safe, if Joel was okay Laney could live with whatever came next. What difference did anything else make as long as those she loved were safe?

That was the thing… She loved Joel. No question.

"I'll check in with you when I return." Victoria waved to someone beyond the glass. "Simon and I have an errand to run."

Laney watched her go.

Thank God for people like Victoria Colby.

Polunsky Prison, 8:00 p.m.

VICTORIA HAD BEEN ESCORTED to the same cold, sterile room as the first time she had met with notorious serial killer Rafe Barker. Warden Prentice had been less than happy with her demand to see his infamous prisoner at this hour, but Victoria had refused to take no for an answer.

In less than three weeks Rafe Barker would be executed for more than a dozen murders. That first time she had come here it had been at his behest. A letter begging her to help him protect his daughters—the daughters he had been accused of murdering twenty-two years ago—had swayed Victoria and brought her here when the warden had insisted she was wasting her time.

Now, almost ten days later, her husband and one of her investigators lay in Beaumont Hospital barely having escaped death. Another man was dead. Janet Tolliver was dead. Fury stoked to a blaze inside Victoria. This had to stop.

Whatever Rafe knew, and she suspected there was a great deal that he wasn't telling her, she would learn now. Or else the agency was washing its hands of this case beyond protecting Sadie, Laney and Olivia.

Each time she thought of how Lucas could have so easily died, she wanted to tear something apart. And that sweet child. Anything could have happened to him today. The child's father, no matter his sins, had been murdered today.

This was enough. No more games.

The door of the interview room opened. Victoria jerked from her troubling thoughts and braced for war. Two prison guards escorted Barker into the room. The leg irons around his ankles and the belly chain coiled about his waist rattled as he was ushered to the chair directly across the table from her just like before. The nylon glides whispered across the tile floor as the chair was drawn back.

"Sit," one of the guards ordered.

Barker followed the instruction given, his gaze already heavy on Victoria. He settled into the molded plastic chair. The second guard secured the leg irons to the floor and the chains on Barker's hands to the underside of the sturdy table that was all that stood between him and Victoria.

"We'll be right outside, ma'am," the first guard said to her, "if you need anything."

"Thank you. We'll be fine."

When the door had closed behind the guards, Barker continued to stare at her, his faded brown eyes dull and listless. "Something happen?"

He had refused to speak to her since her second visit here when she had informed him of how his confidant and nurse, Tony Weeden, had double-crossed him. That he uttered even those two words now surprised her and at the same time infuriated her.

"My husband and one of my investigators were almost killed today. Another man was murdered by your former friend, Tony Weeden. We now have reason to believe he also killed Janet Tolliver."

Barker said nothing. Yet his gaze never deviated from her.

"Your grandson," Victoria said, making this personal, "was abducted by Clare and Tony."

He flinched.

So he wasn't made of stone. "Tony murdered

the child's father and then snatched the little boy with the stench of clotting blood still on his clothes."

Silence.

Victoria braced her hands on the table and leaned forward. Fury had whipped to a frenzy inside her. "What does she want?"

"To finish what I stopped her from doing twenty-two years ago," he uttered in a monotone that made Victoria want to grab him and shake him.

"Weeden took her back to the home the two of you shared. From the looks of things, the intent was to take up residence there again."

The bastard said nothing.

Rage tightened Victoria's lips. "If you know something that will help us stop her, for the love of God, tell me."

Barker leaned forward. Victoria refused to back off.

He stared deep into her eyes. "You can't simply contain her," he whispered. "She's pure evil. I had her contained and they set her free. She won't make the same mistake twice." He leaned away. "Now my daughters will pay the price for the mistake of this so-called justice system."

There was a cryptic message there. "What are you saying?"

He leaned forward again. He waited until she did, as well. Victoria hated the idea of being this close to him.

"The only way to stop her is to kill her." He leaned back far enough to look into her eyes once more. "And I don't think you've got it in you to do that, Victoria." He laughed, a dry rusty sound. "She knows it's you trying to stop her now. And she will do everything in her power to make you pay, too. Trust me, I know."

"She will not stop me," Victoria guaranteed.

Rafe stared at her a moment. "We'll see."

Beaumont Hospital, 9:30 p.m.

WHEN SHE FELT HIS HAND MOVE beneath hers, Laney opened her eyes and sat up straighter. She'd almost dozed off in this uncomfortable old chair.

Joel was watching her.

She smiled. "You're awake." Thank God, thank God. He'd come through the surgery just fine but she wasn't satisfied until he opened those beautiful brown eyes to her.

He managed a lopsided smile. "I dreamed about you."

Her lips trembled at the sound of his voice. His words were so sweet but just hearing him speak made her more happy than any one thing in her entire life except for the birth of her son.

"I hope it was a good dream." She moved to his bedside, took his hand fully in hers.

Uncertainty cluttered his face. "Buddy?"

She glanced at her son curled up on the blanket by her chair. "Sleeping like a rock. He's fine." There was so much she wanted to tell him about how Clare had sent Buddy to her. But that would all have to wait.

Joel released a breath. "Thank God." He looked troubled again. "What about Weeden and Clare?"

She hated to tell him this part. "They got away. But Weeden was injured. So far he hasn't shown up at any clinics or hospitals. As far as we know, anyway."

"I hit him at least once." Joel grimaced. "For a one-armed guy he packs a hell of a blow."

"Are you okay? Do you need more pain medication?" She didn't want him to suffer any more than necessary.

"I'm good." He searched her eyes a moment. "As long as you and Buddy are here, I'm perfect."

More of those sweet words that gave her hope. Laney had done a lot of thinking during the past few hours and she had made some decisions. Maybe they were the wrong ones but there was only one way to find out. "I've been thinking."

He squeezed her hand. "I'm pretty sure you do a lot of that. You're a smart lady."

If he didn't stop she was never going to get all this said. "Anyway, I've decided to sell the house and the saloon and go as far away from here as you're willing to take us."

His gaze held hers but he said nothing. Doubt usurped her confidence, terrified her. Had she read his feelings for her and Buddy wrong?

"You've worked hard on that house and on that saloon, what with all the renovations and building the business. Why would you give that up?"

Well, he'd certainly skirted the real issue. But she couldn't have been that wrong. "If getting out of here ensures that we're all safe, I absolutely will."

For a stretch that felt like a lifetime he searched her eyes some more. "I may be flat on my back right now but I guarantee you I will do a better job of protecting you and Buddy as soon as I'm out of here."

Oh, no. She hadn't meant to make him feel as if any part of what had happened was his failure. Good grief! "But I don't want you to have to protect us like that. I want to be some-place safe."

He tried to rise up on his elbows, grimaced at the effort.

"Wait. Let me raise the bed." Nervous now, she fiddled with the buttons until she was able to raise the head of the bed, putting him in a slightly more upright position. "There."

He wrapped long, strong fingers around hers. "The problem with your plan is that until Weeden and Clare are stopped, they'll keep coming after you. Whether she wants a simple reunion or has some evil agenda, we can't be sure. But her actions indicate the latter. If she only wanted a simple family reunion, mailing out invitations would have done the trick."

Laney thought of how Clare had helped Buddy find her. "If she just wants to see us, why doesn't she say so?"

"That's the part that troubles me. Whatever her reason for approaching the situation like this…it's wrong. We can't take the risk that she'll just give up and go away. We have to square this thing away."

She understood all that. But that wasn't what she meant. Or maybe it was. She was too damned confused. Too exhausted and too scared and worried to beat around the bush.

She wanted to get to the point that had nothing to do with the Barkers.

"I love you, okay?" Oh, God, she'd said it. "I don't want you risking your life to protect us. If that means we have to pull up stakes and move away, that's fine. I'm ready to go."

She'd put her cards on the table.

The longer he stared at her without saying a word, the more she quaked inside.

"Come here." He tugged at her to get her to sit down on the edge of his bed. "I've had a few chicks toss the whole I-love-you thing at me."

Laney's heart sank.

"It was a game and I knew it at the time. Frankly, I always wondered how my brothers had found their soul mates. I thought maybe fate had played a big trick on me."

She wanted to say something but her heart had surged into her throat and she couldn't. She simply couldn't.

"What I do know is that no one has ever offered to give up everything they've worked for just for me." He traced her cheek. "I don't know what I did right to find you or to deserve you and Buddy in my life but I'm sure as hell glad I did."

She tried to hold them back, she really did, but it didn't work. The tears slid down her cheeks.

"I love you, Laney, and I love Buddy. If you let me, I'll spend the rest of my life protecting you."

What was he saying? She'd been so worried about right now she hadn't even thought about the future. "Does that mean you want to take us with you when you go?" That was the closest to a reasonable question she could come up with.

"It means I want to stay here with the two of you."

All the other worries crowded in on her. "If I can't swing that loan we may be on the street." It was the ugly truth.

"You won't need that loan. Not only will we be paying that off but we'll be doing some upgrading."

"You don't have to do all that." She wanted him, not his money.

"I want to do all that, Laney. I want to give you the life you deserve." He swiped at her tears with the backs of his fingers. "And as soon as I'm out of this damned hospital, we're going to find a ring and a minister and we're getting married. Buddy can be my best man."

Laney's breath caught.

"That is, if you'll have me as your husband."

She nodded. "I was hoping you would mention that otherwise I was going to have to do the proposing myself." She felt giddy, wanted to jump for joy.

"We'll have a celebration at the High Noon. We'll have Tatum burn the mortgage in that toaster oven of his."

Laney laughed. "That little incident almost gave the poor guy a nervous breakdown." She'd checked in with him and he had the High Noon under control. "I'm thinking of giving him a raise."

"Make him manager."

Not a bad idea, she thought. "But then what will I do?"

He tugged on a lock of her hair until she leaned down close enough for him to brush a kiss across her lips. "You'll stay home and raise all those babies we're going to have. And watch me teach Buddy how to be the best ball-player in Texas."

She smiled. "Are you suggesting I stay bare-foot and pregnant?"

He grinned. "Only for the first few years."

She raised a skeptical eyebrow. "How about I comanage with Tatum and we'll negotiate the barefoot and pregnant thing? Deal?"

"You drive a hard bargain, ma'am, but you have a deal."

This time he deepened the kiss and Laney

knew for an absolute certainty she had won that negotiation.

Whatever happened from this moment forward, she, Buddy and Joel were a family.

Nothing could stop them.

* * * * *

*Don't miss COLBY ROUNDUP,
the final installment of COLBY, TEXAS,
coming next month only from
Harlequin Intrigue.*

LARGER-PRINT BOOKS!
GET 2 FREE LARGER-PRINT NOVELS PLUS
2 FREE GIFTS!

Harlequin®

INTRIGUE®

BREATHTAKING ROMANTIC SUSPENSE

YES! Please send me 2 FREE LARGER-PRINT Harlequin Intrigue® novels and my 2 FREE gifts (gifts are worth about $10). After receiving them, if I don't wish to receive any more books, I can return the shipping statement marked "cancel." If I don't cancel, I will receive 6 brand-new novels every month and be billed just $5.24 per book in the U.S. or $5.99 per book in Canada. That's a saving of at least 13% off the cover price! It's quite a bargain! Shipping and handling is just 50¢ per book in the U.S. and 75¢ per book in Canada.* I understand that accepting the 2 free books and gifts places me under no obligation to buy anything. I can always return a shipment and cancel at any time. Even if I never buy another book, the two free books and gifts are mine to keep forever.

199/399 HDN FERE

Name _____ (PLEASE PRINT)

Address _____ Apt. #

City _____ State/Prov. _____ Zip/Postal Code

Signature (if under 18, a parent or guardian must sign)

Mail to the **Reader Service:**
IN U.S.A.: P.O. Box 1867, Buffalo, NY 14240-1867
IN CANADA: P.O. Box 609, Fort Erie, Ontario L2A 5X3

Not valid for current subscribers to Harlequin Intrigue Larger-Print books.

**Are you a subscriber to Harlequin Intrigue books
and want to receive the larger-print edition?
Call 1-800-873-8635 today or visit www.ReaderService.com.**

* Terms and prices subject to change without notice. Prices do not include applicable taxes. Sales tax applicable in N.Y. Canadian residents will be charged applicable taxes. Offer not valid in Quebec. This offer is limited to one order per household. All orders subject to credit approval. Credit or debit balances in a customer's account(s) may be offset by any other outstanding balance owed by or to the customer. Please allow 4 to 6 weeks for delivery. Offer available while quantities last.

Your Privacy—The Reader Service is committed to protecting your privacy. Our Privacy Policy is available online at www.ReaderService.com or upon request from the Reader Service.

We make a portion of our mailing list available to reputable third parties that offer products we believe may interest you. If you prefer that we not exchange your name with third parties, or if you wish to clarify or modify your communication preferences, please visit us at www.ReaderService.com/consumerschoice or write to us at Reader Service Preference Service, P.O. Box 9062, Buffalo, NY 14269. Include your complete name and address.

HILP11B

The series you love are now available in

LARGER PRINT!

The books are complete and unabridged—
printed in a larger type size to make it
easier on your eyes.

Harlequin
Romance

From the Heart, For the Heart

Harlequin
INTRIGUE

BREATHTAKING ROMANTIC SUSPENSE

Harlequin
Presents

Seduction and Passion Guaranteed!

Harlequin
Super Romance

Exciting, emotional, unexpected!

Try **LARGER PRINT** today!

Visit: www.ReaderService.com
Call: 1-800-873-8635

Harlequin

A *Romance* FOR EVERY MOOD™

www.ReaderService.com

HLPDIR11

ReaderService.com

You can now manage your account online!

- Review your order history
- Manage your payments
- Update your address

We've redesigned the Reader Service website just for you.

Now you can:

- Read excerpts
- Respond to mailings and special monthly offers
- Learn about new series available to you

Visit us today:

www.ReaderService.com